TANK & FIZZ

THE CASE OF THE SLIME STAMPEDE

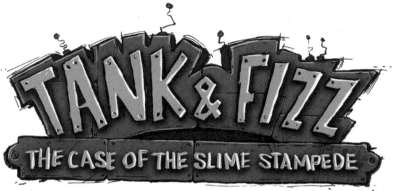

BY

ILLUSTRATED BY

ORCA BOOK PUBLISHERS

Library and Archives Canada Cataloguing in Publication

O'Donnell, Liam, 1970–, author
Tank & Fizz : the case of the slime stampede / Liam O'Donnell; illustrated by Mike Deas.

Issued in print and electronic formats.
ISBN 978-1-4598-0810-2 (pbk.).—ISBN 978-1-4598-0811-9 (pdf).—
ISBN 978-1-4598-0812-6 (epub)

1. Graphic novels. I. Deas, Mike, 1982-, illustrator II. Title.
III. Title: Tank and Fizz.
PN6733.O36T35 2015   j741.5'971   C2014-906602-3
C2014-906603-1

First published in the United States, 2015
Library of Congress Control Number: 2014951651

Summary: A goblin detective and a technology-tinkering troll set out to solve the mystery
of the escaped cleaning slimes.

MIX
Paper from
responsible sources
FSC
www.fsc.org   FSC® C016245

*Orca Book Publishers is dedicated to preserving the environment and
has printed this book on Forest Stewardship Council® certified paper.*

Orca Book Publishers gratefully acknowledges the support for its publishing
programs provided by the following agencies: the Government of Canada through
the Canada Book Fund and the Canada Council for the Arts, and the Province of British
Columbia through the BC Arts Council and the Book Publishing Tax Credit.

Design by Jenn Playford
Illustrations and cover image by Mike Deas

ORCA BOOK PUBLISHERS
www.orcabook.com

Printed and bound in Canada.

19 18 17 16 • 6 5 4 3

For Atticus,
the newest little monster in our clan.
— Liam O'Donnell

For Annie
— Mike Deas

CHAPTER ONE
Slime Surprise

The principal's car got eaten first.

One minute it was sitting in the parking lot, the next it was under a jiggling green slime the size of a school bus. And it wasn't alone.

Slimes covered Gravelmuck Elementary. Globs slurped across the playground. Goopy tentacles wrapped around metal climbing frames. Bubbling puddles lurched through the school's front gates. Green gunk gooped everywhere. It looked like a slag giant with a nasty cold had sneezed on our school.

But I should stick to the facts. Facts are important in my line of work. The name is Fizz Marlow. I'm in fourth grade. I solve mysteries. Hey, it's better than doing homework. Oh, and I'm a goblin. You don't have a thing against goblins, do you? Good.

To a detective like me, facts are like cookies. Choco-slug cookies. Yum.

facts about the
Morning of the **Slimes!**

Fact #1: I got to school early (never doing THAT again!)

Fact #2: The cleaning Slimes had escaped

Fact #3: Principal Weaver's car was dissolved. Not eaten.

Fact number three might be nitpicking, but even a kobold in first grade knows cleaning slimes don't have teeth. They are all about the acid. Sizzling acid that can strip the scales from your back and take the shine out of your wings. Slimes are efficient cleaners. The best in Rockfall Mountain. That's the place we goblins call home.

Slime acid is perfect for getting dried troll boogers off drinking fountains. It scrapes bugbear poop off polished stone floors pretty good too.

This morning, Principal Weaver's front fenders were on the menu. Eaten or dissolved, the effect was the same—no more car. Old Eight-Legs would be walking home today.

Tank was my best friend, troll-tinkerer and detective partner. Now she could add lifesaver to that list. With another slime coming our way, that life didn't look like a long one.

The slime had us cornered on the steps of Mr. Trellik's antique shop. The old troll lived in his shop, which was across the street from our school. He was always yelling at kids to stay away, keep the noise down and basically stop being kids. Rumor had it that the stone statues for sale in his shop were really the remains of children who had got too close to his front door. Tank and I were real close. That didn't seem to bother my best friend.

"That mailbox is made of solid brass," Tank said. She pulled a pair of zoomers over her eyes. She adjusted the dials on the goggles to get a closer look. "No wonder the slime went straight for it."

"And I thought it was because of my sparkling personality."

The door behind us whipped open, totally ruining my witty comeback.

Tank and I both fell backward and landed face to toe with a pair of warty feet.

Mr. Trellik glared down at us.

WHAT ARE YOU TWO BRATS DOING HERE?

CHAPTER TWO

Slimes and Spiders

"**W**hatever it is you're selling, I don't want it!" Mr. Trellik snapped.

The old troll was the color of slug soup. Steam drifted up from the tiny teacup in his large hand. One fact about Mr. Trellik—the old troll loves his tea. Mr. Trellik's eyes nearly popped out of his bald head when he saw the massive slime at the bottom of his stairs.

"My mailbox!" he shrieked. He marched down the stairs, shaking his teacup at the slime. "You filthy brute! How dare you eat my property!"

"Careful, Mr. Trellik!" boomed a deep voice from the other side of the street.

Mr. Snag, our school caretaker, ran across the road. He carried a long toolbox in his big hands. The large ogre was out of breath. His round belly heaved in and out.

It looked like a mud ball getting pumped up and deflated over and over again.

"My slimes ain't filthy," Mr. Snag said when he caught his breath. "Don't be hurting their feelings."

"Feelings!" Mr. Trellik spat. "These blobs are barely alive. They certainly don't have ears, and I doubt they have feelings."

"That might be true, but you don't have to go and say it. Besides, my slimes can't resist the taste of such high-quality brass."

Mr. Trellik took a sip of his tea, considering Mr. Snag's words.

"I do only use the finest materials." He narrowed his eyes. "Don't you butter me up, you old ogre! Get that slime off my mailbox before I call the police!"

Judging from the sirens in the distance, the cops were already on their way. Mr. Snag's large ears drooped down the sides of his hairy head like a pair of sad wings.

Poor Mr. Snag. He was always cleaning up other people's messes. He got your ball down when an older monster roofed it. He unblocked the toilet when Rizzo Rawlins and his goons jammed it with toilet paper or some unlucky first-grader. This mess was different.

All caretakers in Slick City need a license to use cleaning slimes. There are strict laws on who can control slimes. In the wrong hands or left to slurp around on its own, a slime could cause a lot of damage. My school's dissolved playground was proof of that. And so was Mr. Snag's worried face.

Mr. Snag was in charge of the slimes at Gravelmuck Elementary. He watched over them like they were his own children. This mess was his mess.

The ogre pulled a small glass cube out of his toolbox. He tapped the cube. It hummed and grew bigger, until it was the size of a backpack. When it had finished growing, Mr. Snag held a solid-looking glass box. One side of the cube opened like a door.

Mr. Snag held the glass box closer for us to see. "This ain't magic," he said. "It's the finest in trollish engineering."

Tank's troll ears perked up. She was an aspiring engineer. To her, Mr. Snag's boxes were like candy to a double-mouthed sugar sucker.

"Are those sunken pistons?" she said.

Mr. Snag grinned. "And invisible gearing. A machine so perfect, it beats magic in every way."

Mr. Snag placed the box on the ground beside the blob. He reached into one of the many pockets on his red coveralls and pulled out a small piece of dark stone.

"Obsidian." He winked. "Slimes cannot resist the taste of obsidian."

He dropped the obsidian pieces into the box. Immediately, the slime oozed toward the black stone.

"Can it smell it?" I said.

Mr. Snag shook his head. "Slimes don't have noses, Fizz. They feel the vibrations of stones. It's like they can hear rocks. And when they hear obsidian, they come slurping."

The slime totally forgot about Mr. Trellik's brass mailbox. It poured itself onto the obsidian and into the glass box. Amazingly, the box was able to hold the entire slime's body.

"Another feat of engineering." Mr. Snag grinned. "Tiny pistons in the box's lining massage the slime and make it shrink to fit in the box."

He pushed the lid closed with one large foot and picked up the glass box. Inside, the slime happily devoured the chunk of obsidian like it was a candy-coated rock bug.

"Won't the slime's acids just eat through the glass?" I asked.

Mr. Snag's large ears wiggled with delight. "That's the beauty of it! The glass is actually made from refined slick."

"The goop sucked up from under the harbor?"

"The very stuff," Mr. Snag said. "Slimes can't stand the stuff, so they don't eat it."

The slime's body squished up against the glass of the tiny box. Already, the piece of obsidian was smaller.

"Impressive," I said.

Mr. Trellik snorted. "I'll be more impressed when these beasts are gone from the front of my shop! I have a very important shipment coming today. I cannot have slimes here to greet my customers."

The old troll pointed to a poster hanging beside the door to his antique shop.

"Firebane!" I said. "The dragon from the Dark Depths?"

"The very one." Mr. Trellik grinned. "He has come upon hard times and chosen to sell off some of his estate."

"You mean, ill-gotten loot," Mr. Snag said. "That old dragon has terrorized the good people of Rockfall Mountain for centuries."

"That is not my place to say." Mr. Trellik shrugged. "I'll have the wealthiest monsters from all over Rockfall Mountain visiting my store this weekend. Slimes are *not* invited!"

I peeked inside his shop. The place was packed with old furniture, parts of ships and display cases of gems and jewelry. The floors were black as the Dark Depths and polished to a shine. I'd never been inside, but it looked like a fun place to get lost. If Mr. Trellik wasn't around, that is.

"It's a good thing the slimes didn't get a look at the floor inside the shop," I whispered to Tank.

"Obsidian," she said. The floor tiles of Trellik's shop were made of the slimes' favorite treat. "You can't cut through that stuff. All the banks are built out of it. It is expensive, but very secure."

"And delicious if you're a slime," I said.

A shadow fell across the front of the antique shop.
A voice bellowed from above.
"Do not panic!"

"You're making a big mistake!" I shouted. Not like that was going to stop the police from stuffing Mr. Snag into their car.

"You've got the wrong ogre!" Tank said.

Something was definitely wrong. I felt it right down to my tail. And a good detective knows to listen to his tail. I ran down the steps to the police car.

"Mr. Snag loves his cleaning beasts," I said to the cop holding the car door open. "He would never let them escape like this."

"That's nice, kid." The cop smiled like I was some first-grader bragging about losing a fang. He pushed Mr. Snag into the backseat of the car. "Your caretaker has keys to both the slime cages and the front door of the school. We know what we're doing."

"Zip it, Osborne!" A large ogre in a rumpled overcoat came around from the other side of the car. He looked like he washed his face in lemon juice. "This is a police investigation, not show-and-tell with the kiddies."

Osborne's grin vanished. "Sorry, Detective Hordish."

Hordish turned to us.

"Keep your snouts out of my investigation, kids." He waved Tank and I away with a big meaty hand. "Now run along. I'm sure you have homework to finish."

Hordish and Osborne climbed into their police car. Mr. Snag stared out at us through the back window.

The caretaker's long ears hung down the sides of his hairy face. His large eyes stared out at the school he had taken care of since before Tank and I were even born. Slime damage was everywhere—cars dissolved, fences melted away and the playground filled with puddles of slime acid. It was a mess, and Mr. Snag was going to take the blame.

The police car roared to life and sped downtown to the police station.

"This ain't right, Fizz," Tank muttered through gritted teeth. "Mr. Snag would never hurt the school or his slimes like this. We have to do something."

"We are," I said. "We're going to find out who really released the slimes."

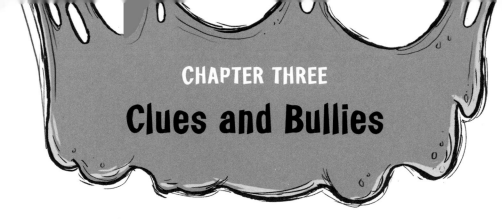

CHAPTER THREE
Clues and Bullies

Recess stinks when your playground is a crime scene. After the police hauled Mr. Snag away, Principal Weaver led us all back into our school. The teachers tried to teach as usual. Outside, the police cleaned up the remaining slimes from the schoolyard. When the recess bell rang, we got a closer look at the damage.

Gravelmuck was a mess. The parking lot was full of holes and half-eaten cars. The slides and climbing equipment were a mangled mess of metal.

The police had wrapped half of the schoolyard in fat yellow Do Not Cross tape. Every ogre, troll and goblin from kindergarten to grade eight was shoved into one corner of the playground. That didn't leave a lot of room to stretch your wings or swing your tail. The duty teachers were pretty busy breaking up accidental clawings and the not-so-accidental scorchings.

With Mr. Snag taken away by the cops, I wasn't really in the mood for recess anyway. I had a mystery to solve. Tank and I have been solving mysteries since kindergarten. We've cracked many cases around our school, from missing tail-warmers to lost lunches. Clearing Mr. Snag's name was definitely going to be our biggest challenge so far.

With the teachers busy running crowd control, Tank and I had our chance to dig for some clues. Thanks to Officer Osborne's loose lips, we knew the slimes had escaped through the front door of the school. The question was, how did they get through the door?

Thankfully, Tank always came to school prepared. I'm not talking about pencils-and-paper prepared. I'm talking troll-tinkering, network-hacking prepared. As a junior engineer, Tank is never without her tool belt. I don't pretend to know how half the stuff works. From sonic hatchdrivers to pocket-sized spectroscopic enhancers, Tank is the troll with the tools.

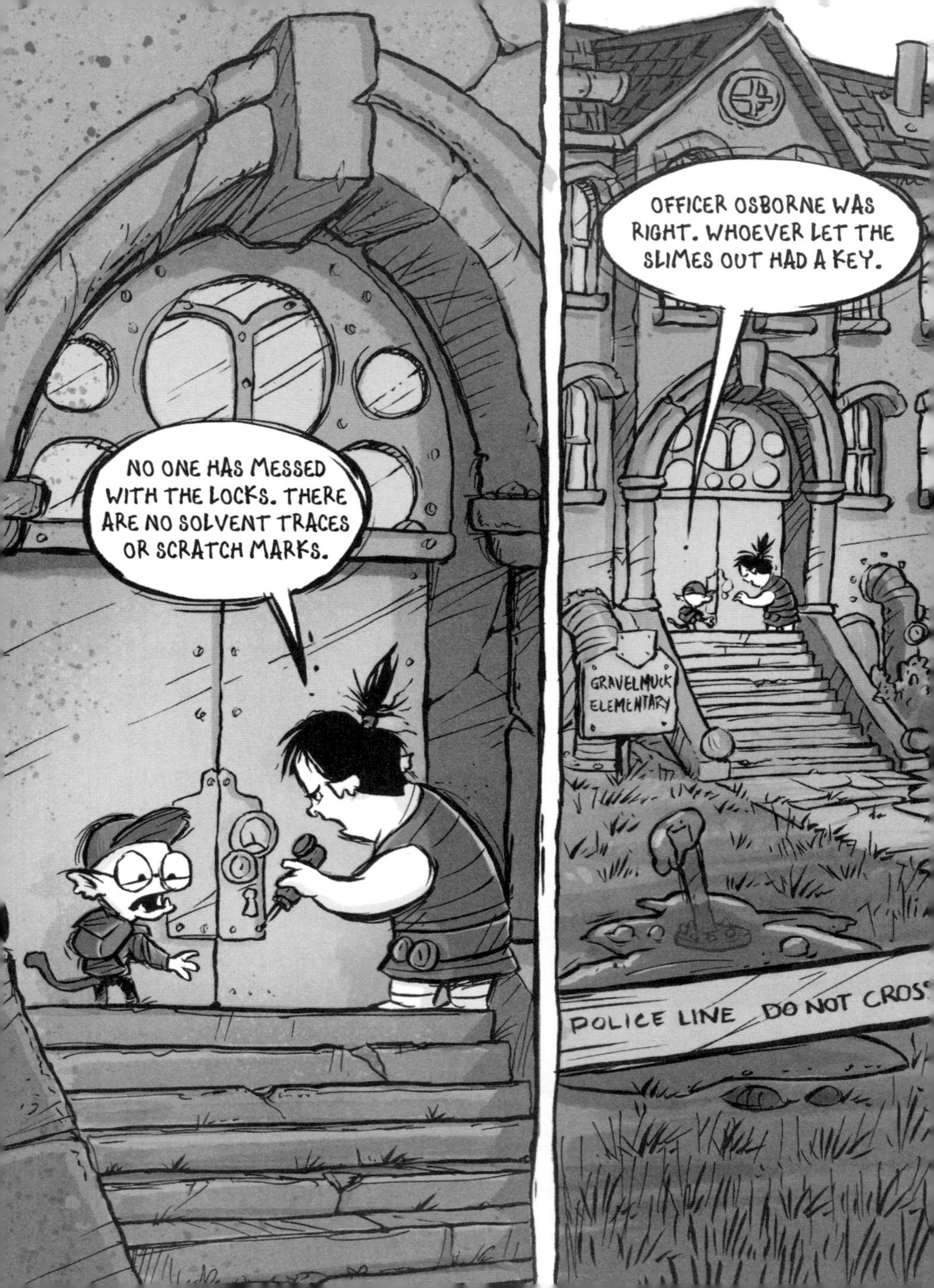
NO ONE HAS MESSED WITH THE LOCKS. THERE ARE NO SOLVENT TRACES OR SCRATCH MARKS.
OFFICER OSBORNE WAS RIGHT. WHOEVER LET THE SLIMES OUT HAD A KEY.
GRAVELMUCK ELEMENTARY
POLICE LINE DO NOT CROS

"Mr. Snag would definitely have the key," Tank said. "You still think he's innocent?"

"My tail thinks so," I said. "And you know what I always say."

"Yeah, yeah. Smart detectives always listen to their tails."

It was getting late. Recess would be over soon. I ducked under the police tape to grab what little recess was left.

Instead, something grabbed me. Two somethings, actually.

A pair of burly ogre hands lifted me off the ground. An identical pair held Tank in place. Identical hands for identical twins. The Gutro brothers, Seymor and Julius. Two of the meanest grade-seven ogres you'll ever meet. These two don't bother shaking down the kindergartners for lunch money—they shake down the teachers. A bigger payoff for a pair of big goons.

"Look what we caught," Seymor said.

"A couple of snoopy snoops," Julius said, finishing his brother's sentence. They did that all the time. It was like they shared a brain, which seemed about right. They definitely didn't each have one of their own.

"Principal Weaver will not be pleased," said the little dog-faced kobold standing with the twins.

Rizzo Rawlins. The nastiest kobold in the whole school district and the one giving the orders to the Gutro brothers. Rizzo was small even for a kobold, but his family's money made him a lot bigger.

Like all kobolds, Rizzo was covered in patchy orange and black fur. He had beady little eyes and sour breath that could peel the crust off a dung dweller's backside. He moved in close and gave me a full whiff.

"Let us go, Rizzo," Tank said. "We're not bothering you."

"Not so fast!" Rizzo barked. Literally. When the guy spoke, half his words came out as barks. That's kobolds for you. "Your friend Mr. Snag is in a lot of trouble. And he deserves it."

"You're just mad because he caught you writing love poems in the boys' washroom last week," I said.

"They weren't poems!" Rizzo said. His fur bristled around his face. "They were warnings to snoops like you. Rizzo Rawlins runs this school. You go snooping around these halls, you got to check with me first."

"You know something about the escaped slimes, Rizzo?" Tank asked.

"What I know and what I tell trolls like you are two very different things."

"The bell's going to ring, Rizzo." I tried to wriggle free of Seymor's grip. I might as well have tried to lift the school. "Let's go inside and discuss this like real monsters."

"There's nothing to discuss, Fizzle," Rizzo snarled. My scales stiffened at the sound of that nickname. "Mr. Snag caused this mess and now he's going to pay. It's about time we got rid of those dangerous slimes.

A little kid could get hurt with them slurping around the school."

"Since when did you care about little kids?" Tank asked.

Rizzo's furry hand went to his heart, like he'd been shot by an arrow. "I'm all about standing up for the little guy."

"That's 'cause you are a little guy, boss!" Seymor said. The ogre's face lit up like he'd just discovered Firebane's hidden hoard.

"Zip it! I'm not paying you to make wisecracks." Rizzo flashed his sharp teeth. The ogres swallowed their laughter and tightened their grips on us. Rizzo's beady eyes snapped back to me. "Things will be better with old Snag gone, Fizz. Leave it that way. Got it?"

Before I could throw out a zinger that would put the kobold in his place, Rizzo snapped his fingers. The Gutro brothers spun into action. And I mean really spun.

Seymor grabbed the yellow police tape and wrapped it around my arms. He picked me up and spun me so fast that the tape wrapped me from head to toe. He plopped me on the ground beside Tank. Julius had given her the spin cycle treatment too. We were both wrapped up like a pair of yellow burritos.

The recess bell rang, ending our fifteen minutes of freedom. Kids rushed back to their classes. Tank and I squirmed but didn't get far.

Rizzo and his goons gave us one last snarly command before they went inside. "Stop your slime-snooping. Let old Snag get the punishment he deserves. Trust me. It's better for everyone this way."

"Everyone but Mr. Snag!" Tank said.

"I'd be more worried about yourselves right now. Principal Weaver gets her web warped when little monsters are late for class."

Rizzo and his goons marched back into the school, laughing the whole way.

Watching them go, I was certain about two things. Rizzo knew something about the escaped slimes. And we were going to be late for class.

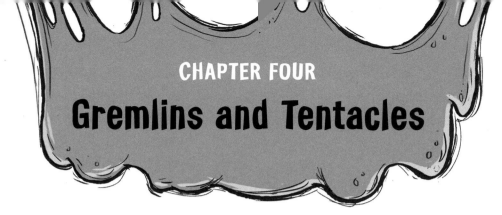

CHAPTER FOUR
Gremlins and Tentacles

Downtown Slick City was busier than a school cafeteria serving candied leeches. Monsters crowded the sidewalks. Cars jammed the streets. Trolls, goblins and ogres all headed home from a long day of work.

Home is where I wanted to be too. My stomach rumbled. I was missing my afternoon appointment with a plate of choco-slug cookies. I reminded my stomach that I was on a case. I had to focus. My stomach grumbled some more. Clearly, it didn't understand detective work.

Being wrapped up in police tape gave me time to think. We needed to talk to Mr. Snag and get his side of the story.

Tank and I were eventually freed from Rizzo's tape job by a troll in grade eight. She got to school late and missed all the slimy fun but was kind enough to unravel two stuck fourth-graders. Our teacher, Mr. Mantle, was so busy boring the other students with geometry, he didn't even notice us slip into class late. A lucky break that saved Tank and I from detention and kept our investigation on track. Best of all, we missed Mr. Mantle's homework walk, where he struts around the classroom looking at the math questions we did the night before. Or, in my case, *didn't* do the night before. For the record, homework and me don't get along.

Anyway, there we were, standing under the shadow of the Slick City police station in the middle of rush hour. With my mom.

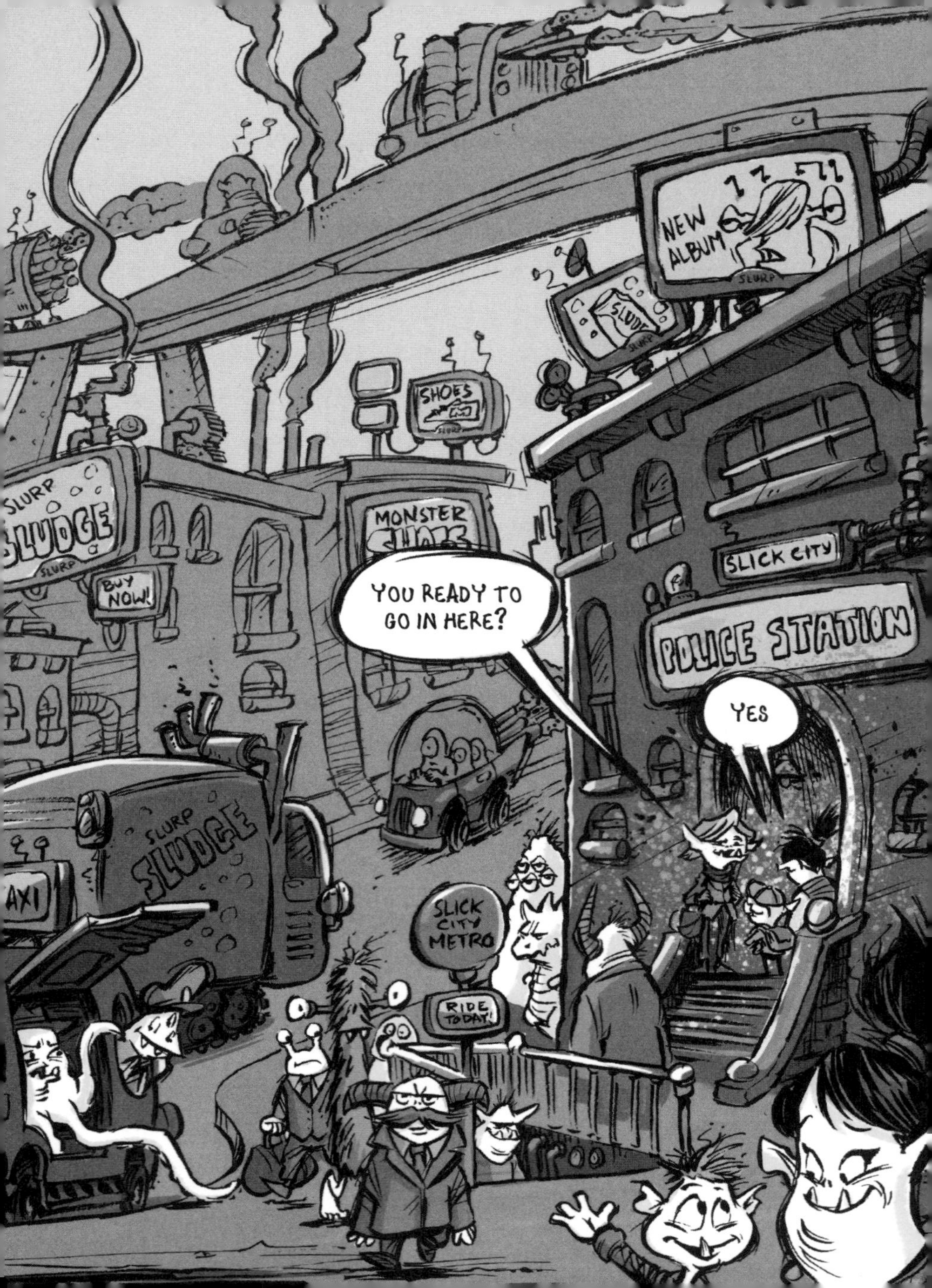
NEW ALBUM
SLURP
SHOES
SLURP SLUDGE
BUY NOW!
MONSTER
SLICK CITY
POLICE STATION
YOU READY TO GO IN HERE?
YES
SLURP SLUDGE
SLICK CITY METRO
RIDE TODAY!

My mom's a reporter for the *Rockfall Times*. Perhaps you've read it. Maybe you've lined your budgie's cage with it. I recommend the comics section. My mom actually reads the articles. What can I say? Grown-ups are weird.

"Lucky for you, I was coming down here today anyway," she said as she led us through the front doors. "I have to talk to the chief for my latest story. Word is, the Gremlin Gang is coming to Slick City."

Tank scowled. "Gremlins? Since when do gremlins come here? Slick City is near the sea. Gremlins hate water. They usually stay away from port cities."

"I'm hoping the police can answer that question," Mom said.

Inside the station, it was like someone had opened a can of chaos. Police officers of all shapes, sizes and fur colors scurried and shuffled through the large reception room. Officers returned from patrolling the streets, looking haggard and tired. A few dragged sad-looking culprits of petty crimes along with them. Slick City is a nice place to live, but that doesn't mean we don't have a few rotten turnips. A big desk on a platform at the back loomed over the crowded room. A large purple octo-ettin sat behind the desk.

Thick tentacles sprouted from her trunk-like body. Each tentacle was busy doing a different job. Two tentacles put thick brown folders into a dented filing cabinet. Another two typed quickly on a computer keyboard. Another tentacle held a phone to the officer's ear. Two more tentacles poured sugar into a steaming cup of what looked like a much-needed tea.

"Busy enough for you, Gladis?" Mom said to the octo-ettin.

"Just another day at the office, Rana." Gladis hung up the phone. She raised her teacup with one tentacle and took a long sip of tea while her other tentacles carried on working. "Detective Hordish said you'd be coming."

Tank's eyes snapped to mine at the mention of the detective's name. Hordish was one of the ogres who had hauled Mr. Snag away.

"I'm here to find out the latest on the Gremlin Gang," Mom said.

"They're the biggest news on the wires right now." Gladis rolled her large single eye. "A gang of little blue critters running around Rockfall Mountain robbing museums, art galleries and anywhere else with some-thing to steal. They've committed three robberies in three weeks."

"And each robbery in a town not far from Slick City," Mom added. "You think they're heading this way?"

"What do I know? I only answer the phones around here." Gladis's eye looked at Tank and me. "Hordish didn't say anything about adorable kiddies visiting!"

Two tentacles took a break from filing and stretched over her desk down to us. Gladis gave Tank and I a playful tickle behind the ear. That's something adults do. I don't get it, but it makes them happy, so whatever.

"They're here to visit their school caretaker, Thaxlin Snag. Is that okay?"

"Don't see why not," Gladis said. "The old fella is allowed visitors. He seemed so sad when they brought him in this morning. It's a crime to have him locked up in here. That poor ogre wouldn't hurt a pixie flea."

As she spoke, Gladis stretched out a free tentacle and grabbed a young goblin officer by the arm. She pulled the startled goblin across the floor to us like she was reeling in a fish.

"Declan," she growled at the goblin, her thick tentacle still around his wrist. "Quit your daydreaming and bring these two fine children to see Mr. Snag in Visiting Room B."

CHAPTER FIVE

Snag Speaks

Declan led us through a heavy door and down a long corridor. He ushered us into a small room with a table and three chairs around it.

"Wait here," he said and disappeared out the door.

A few minutes later, the goblin returned with Mr. Snag at his side.

The caretaker's face was pale and his thick hair matted and standing up on one side. He'd been locked up for less than a day, but already he looked years older.

"Tank! Fizz!" His wide smile couldn't hide the weariness in his eyes. He slumped into the chair on the other side of the table. "Nice of you to visit an old troll in trouble."

"We want to help you, Mr. Snag," I said.

"You didn't release the slimes, did you?" Tank asked.

"Of course not! They're like my children." He shook his head. "My poor slimes."

"Tell us what happened," I said. I pulled out my detective notebook. Really, it's my math homework book, but not a lot of math gets done in it. Like I said, homework and I don't see eye to eye.

Mr. Snag sat up straight. "I locked up the school as usual. I went home, read a book and went to sleep. When I got to school in the morning, the slimes were already slurping around the playground."

"Was there anyone with you at home last night?" Tank asked. "If someone was with you, that would prove you didn't come to school in the night and release the slimes."

Mr. Snag shook his head. "Nope. Just me and a good book."

There went that alibi.

"Did you lock the door when you left the school?" I asked.

"Like I always do. Double-checked it and everything." Mr. Snag didn't hesitate with his answer.

"The lock on the front door was not tampered with," Tank said. "Whoever let the slimes out had their own key."

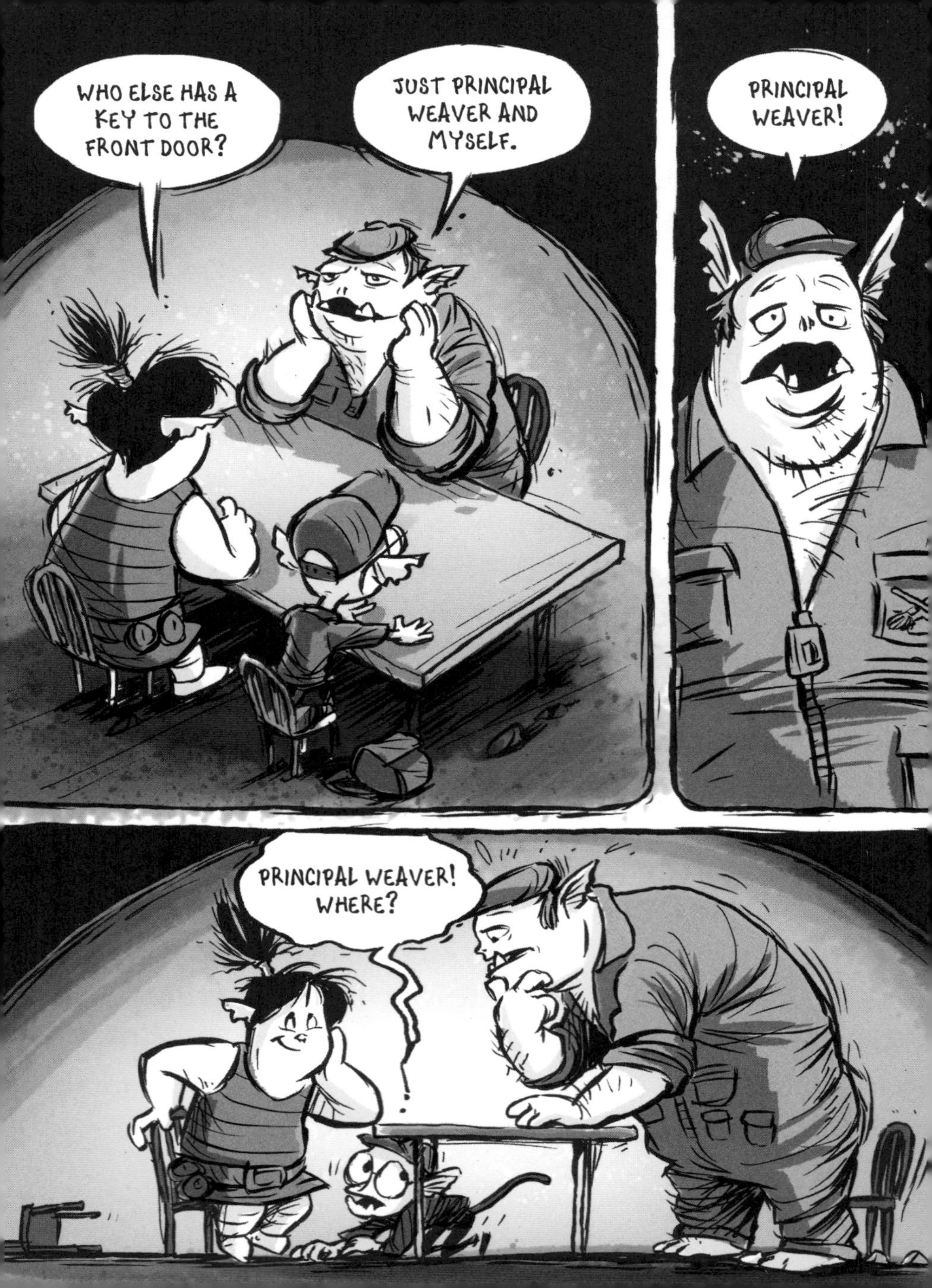
WHO ELSE HAS A KEY TO THE FRONT DOOR?
JUST PRINCIPAL WEAVER AND MYSELF.
PRINCIPAL WEAVER!
PRINCIPAL WEAVER! WHERE?

Mr. Snag chuckled. "She's not here, silly goblin." Then he got serious again. "Principal Weaver is behind this mess. She let the slimes out!"

"Why would she do that?"

"To get rid of me." Mr. Snag's voice sounded hollow. He paused, like he had a story to tell. I pulled my seat closer. I like a good story. "It started last week, with that visitor. A big fella, long ears, wide mouth. All teeth and promises. He wanted to speak to the monster in charge. I brought him to Weaver's office. This fella said he was with a cleaning company and he wanted to clean our school."

"A cleaning company?" Tank said. "But the school uses you guys from the Guild of Cleaners."

"There's no finer group of caretakers in all of Rockfall Mountain. The Guild of Cleaners has kept this city clean since the first barrels of slick were hauled out of Fang Harbor." Mr. Snag touched the guild crest on his red overalls. The little patch showed two mops crossed like swords over a cute-looking slime. "This big lumbering oaf said he was cheaper than the guild. He said he was going to clean the school with…machines." Mr. Snag said the last word like it hurt for it to travel over his tongue. "You know I love a good piece of engineering, but a machine will never clean as good as a slime."

"Principal Weaver sent him packing, right?" I scribbled in my notebook as fast as my pencil would go. That's not very fast, but I was getting most of the details.

Mr. Snag shook his head. "She was ready to hug him with all eight of her legs."

I shivered at the thought of a hug from Principal Weaver.

"The Guild of Cleaners has a contract with all the schools in Slick City," Tank said. "Principal Weaver can't bring in a new cleaner and get rid of you."

"That's what I told her," Mr. Snag said. "It only made her more angry with me."

"If she had a reason to get rid of you, then she could hire someone new," Tank said.

"You think Weaver released the slimes to get you in trouble?" I said.

Mr. Snag nodded. "Seems pretty obvious to me."

"It would definitely explain how the slimes got out of the school."

The caretaker's ears drooped. "My poor slimes. Are they okay? Who's taking care of them?"

The slimes! We'd been so busy looking for clues, we hadn't thought about what happened to Mr. Snag's slimes.

The last I'd seen of them, the police were packing them into containers. After that, who knew?

Mr. Snag's big eyes were red, and he seemed one sniffle away from crying. "Those slimes need me. Who is going to feed them? You've got to make sure they're okay."

"We will, Mr. Snag. Don't worry," I said. "We'll find your slimes and catch the monster who let them loose."

I hoped I sounded like I knew what I was doing, because I didn't.

This was our biggest case yet. It was way bigger than finding lost lunches for first-graders. With Principal Weaver as our prime suspect, Tank and I were dancing with big danger too. If we messed this up, we would be stuck in detention for the rest of our lives. Or, worse, sentenced to a lifetime membership in the Math Club.

CHAPTER SIX
Caught in Weaver's Web

The next morning, I still didn't have a plan and we still didn't have a schoolyard. Half-eaten swing sets and climbing frames were piled into one corner against the mostly dissolved fence. It looked like a giant acid-drooling baby had had a giant tantrum.

Tank was at our usual morning meeting place, at the side of the school, near the bike racks. Actually, where the bike racks *used* to be. Now there was just a large black patch of scorched rock and a pile of twisted metal. Slimes are messy eaters.

GET OVER HERE, FIZZ. YOU'RE MISSING ALL THE ACTION.

IT'S TOO EARLY FOR ACTION.

SEE FOR YOURSELF, DETECTIVE.

"Big deal," I said. "The cafeteria is getting their shipment of mystery meat. Compared with yesterday's slime attack, this doesn't really rate as *action,* Tank."

"It's not meat, meathead. Read the label on that box."

"So, the school is getting a new dishwasher," I said. "It's a thrill a minute around here today."

"That's not a dishwasher, Fizz. It's a vacuum cleaner."

"Sorry. My mistake." Then it hit me. "Why is the school getting a new vacuum cleaner? We have Mr. Snag and his slimes."

"Correction. We *had* Mr. Snag and his slimes," Tank said. "Then things got slimy."

"Look who they're buying it from," I said.

Tank read the name on the side of the delivery truck.

"Rawlins' Deal Depot. Rizzo's family business." Rawlins' Deal Depot was a chain of stores that sold everything from vacuums to baby food. They had sprouted up on every corner, spreading across Slick City like a virus. Monsters from all over the mountain bought their furniture and appliances from Rawlins' Deal Depot. It made the Rawlins clan one of the richest families in the mountain. And it made Rizzo think he could boss around every other monster like one of his employees.

The morning bell rang, calling us back to class. Five minutes later, we were stampeding into school like good little monsters. Running, screaming, yelling. You know, a typical start to the school day.

We bounced down the corridor, past Mrs. Trogeltusk's kindergarten class and into the main office. We slid past the school secretary's desk.

"Morning, Mr. Granger," I said. I tried to sound like sliding on your butt backward is a totally normal thing to be doing at school first thing in the morning.

"Watch where you're being dragged! Don't damage my floors." The old fire skeleton's flaming eyeballs flared in their sockets. "Hurry up. She's expecting you."

Principal Weaver's office was more like a cave. The dark kind that haunts your dreams.

A feeble glowshroom gave off only enough light to fill the room with shadows. Sticky webs covered the walls and ceiling. Against the far wall, three small cocoons dangled. Unlucky students serving morning detention, or Weaver's lunch? It was hard to tell with Old Eight-Legs.

We skidded to a stop in front of the principal's desk.

My heart pounded so hard, I thought it was going to burst from my chest and run screaming down the corridor. I couldn't blame it. My eyes adjusted to the darkness. Goblins' eyes work well in dim light, but in here, I could see little more than shadows.

"Welcome, children." A voice from the dark. Principal Weaver. I'd recognize her hissing anywhere. "It's time we had a little chat."

CHAPTER SEVEN
New Caretakers and Deal Makers

My heart pounded like an ogre's war drum. My gut felt like I'd eaten half a lava pie.

"I've been looking for you two little monsters," Principal Weaver said.

"Let me guess. You'd like us to read tomorrow's morning announcements?" I said with a weak laugh.

"Save the jokes for the playground, Fizz Marlow," Weaver snapped.

The webs along the walls behind her shivered when she spoke. Dark shapes skittered around the ceiling. Behind the webs, Weaver's spider babies lurked. Hundreds of them, scurrying through the school. Watching and reporting back to Mommy. The whole room was alive with them. Alive and hungry.

"You were close to our old caretaker, Mr. Snag." Principal Weaver stretched her words out longer than a math lesson on a Friday afternoon. "But after his carelessness, he simply couldn't be trusted. So he had to be let go."

"It wasn't his fault," Tank said. She struggled against the sticky web around her arms. "There's no proof he let the slimes out."

Weaver sighed. "I know you both like to investigate things. Like a pair of nosy little gossips."

"Um, we prefer detectives," I said before I could bite down on my runaway tongue.

"Silence!" Weaver zipped up to her web sharply. Behind her, the ceiling and walls shuddered. Her babies did not like it when Mommy got mad. "No more snooping around, you two. Mr. Snag is gone from our school. He brought it on himself with those terrifying beasts."

Tank's eyes widened at the mention of the cleaning slimes. "What have you done with them?"

"Don't worry about those filthy globs of goo," Weaver said. "You should be more concerned about what Mommy and Daddy will say if I catch you using your gadgets again to snoop around my school."

The principal smiled when she saw the surprise on my face.

"Yes, little Fizz," she hissed. "We saw you poking around the front door yesterday."

We? A shiver ran down my tail. Weaver's spy-babies had watched us investigate the lock during recess. My heart shrank at the thought of those little spiders watching our every move.

Principal Weaver dropped down from her web and tapped me on the snout with one of her long legs.

"Forget the cleaning beasts, Fizz. Forget Mr. Snag. And forget we ever had this little chat." The spider's red eyes locked onto me. "Agreed?"

We agreed. What else could we do? Being stuck to the floor with a venomous principal hanging over your head will make anyone agreeable.

"Good!" Principal Weaver zipped back up her thread. "I'm glad that's settled. You may return to class."

The webs on the walls around us shivered. A dozen baby spiders, skittered out from the walls. They crawled over us, snipping away at the web with their delicate arms. In seconds, we were free from the sticky web. The spiders scurried back into the shadows. The walls quivered as they burrowed back into their homes.

As we turned to make our getaway, there was a knock on the door.

ANYONE HOME?

Principal Weaver picked her way across the webbing on the wall. "Like I told you, Mr. Snag is out. Mr. Zallin is in. It's really not that difficult to understand, children."

Mr. Zallin lumbered into the room. He walked slowly, as if he had to really think about every step he took. Maybe he was nervous around Principal Weaver too.

"Nice to meet you, kids," Mr. Zallin said. His voice sounded like boulders crashing down a cliff. His fierce yellow eyes met each of ours. It was like he was memorizing our faces for a test. Then he broke into a wide smile. "You can call me Zal!"

Zal wore a pair of blue grease-stained overalls and large work boots. Around his waist was a wide tool belt with many pockets. A different metal gadget poked out of each pocket.

Tank's eyes went wide at the sight of the flashing gizmos in Zal's belt.

"Is that a tronic biohammer?" she asked. Her hand reached out to the fat metal tweezers topped with a spinning jewel.

"Yes, it is," Zal said. He took the tool out of his belt to show Tank. "It's very handy."

"Much more useful than those silly cleaning slimes." Principal Weaver buzzed around her web like it was charged with electricity. "Zal will be a much better caretaker than Mr. Snag and his nasty beasts. I'm sure you will show him how helpful we are at Gravelmuck Elementary."

"Whatever you say, Principal Weaver," I mumbled.

I pulled Tank out of Weaver's office before she could ask Zal more questions about his electro-bio whatever-it-was. Halfway back to class, I yanked her to a stop.

"You don't really think Zal is a better caretaker than Mr. Snag. Do you?"

She didn't answer. This was bad. Tank was in a tool trance.

"Tank, snap out of it!"

"What?" She looked around the corridor like she'd woken from a dream. A happy dream with flashing lights and whirring gizmos. Her face darkened when she saw it was me who'd woken her from her dream. "Look, Fizz, maybe Zal isn't such a bad guy after all. Machines are better than cleaning beasts—everyone knows that."

"What?" I lowered my voice so Weaver's spies scurrying along the walls could not hear. "Have you forgotten about Mr. Snag? He's stuck in jail and his slimes have vanished. We promised to get him out, remember?"

"Sure, sure, whatever." Her voice sounded distant. Then her eyes lit up. "Hey, I wonder if Zal would let me peek under the hood of his Clean-o-Tron XL.

I bet it uses a quad-core, slick-injection motor. I haven't seen one of those up close before."

She walked away muttering about circuits and biometric something-or-others.

This was bad. First I'd lost our school caretaker. Was I losing my detective partner too?

SCRITCH
SCRITCH

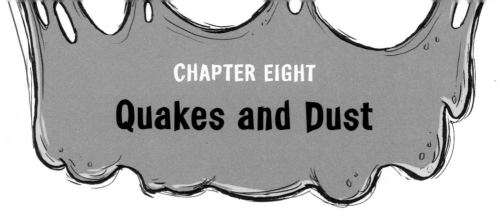

CHAPTER EIGHT

Quakes and Dust

The rest of the day dragged like a legless zombie tied to a dump truck. History class oozed into drama, which limped into science and eventually crashed into math.

And that's where Mr. Mantle was setting a record for the most boring lesson ever. Old Tentacle-Face droned on about convex and acute angles. I never met an angle I thought was cute.

Angles were on my mind though. Not the math kind of angles. Detective angles, reasons why someone commits a crime, filled my brain. Who let the slimes out? Why was Principal Weaver so quick to get rid of Mr. Snag and his cleaning beasts? She said she was saving money with Mr. Zallin. Did she ruin the poor ogre's career to save a few bucks? And where did all the slimes go? No one had given us a straight answer on that one. Just like my math work, things weren't adding up.

The entire classroom started to shake.

Dust dropped from the ceiling, desks clattered together, books bounced off shelves. Then the shaking stopped.

"Everyone stay calm," Mr. Mantle said. "It's just Rockfall Mountain letting us know it's here." His tentacles danced a jig on his face. He was definitely struggling to stay calm.

Considering that we lived underground in a mountain, tremors like this were not unusual. But usually the shaking wasn't bad enough to knock stuff to the ground.

High on the wall above the chalkboard, the PA speaker crackled to life.

"ATTENTION! ATTENTION!" Principal Weaver's shrill voice pierced the classroom. I settled into my seat, ready for another rambling message from our great leader. "Your attention, please! You may have noticed a slight shaking. Do not be alarmed. Our new caretaker, the wonderful Mr. Zallin, is running some tests on our heating system. That is the cause of the minor shaking. He tells me it will continue over the next few days. That is all."

The PA speaker let out a final, ear-splitting crackle and then went quiet. The entire class sat in silence for a moment. Silence, that is, except for the quiet drip of water.

A river of clear liquid rolled from under the seats to the front of the class.

"Oops," Ranatha Allabara said, blushing. Blue-fin waterloks are 98 percent seawater, and she was leaking a good 20 percent of that all over the classroom floor. The tremor had torn the thin lining around her waist. She worked quickly at the tears with a sharp needle and thread. "Don't worry—I can fix it."

Mr. Mantle peered at the puddle on the floor. "Yes, but who is going to fix the mess on my floor?"

"We will," I said. I grabbed Tank and had her on her feet before Mr. Mantle knew what was happening. "We'll get a mop from Mr. Snag, er, I mean, Mr. Zallin. Be right back!"

We were out the door and on our way to the basement before Mr. Mantle had time to give us permission.

Tank stopped me at the top of the stairs.

"Okay, when did Fizz Marlow become Helpful Goblin of the Month?"

"When he realized he needed to see Mr. Snag's office," I said. "Everyone is ready to get rid of him and I want to know why."

"And you think we might find something in his office in the basement?"

"It's worth a shot. I also want to check on the slime cages he had down there. No one knows where those poor slimes went after they escaped. And, worse, no one cares."

The school basement was dark and empty. No sign of Zal and no sign of the slimes. Few kids liked coming down here, but I didn't mind it. I liked dropping by to feed Mr. Snag's slimes leftovers from my lunch. There's something soothing about a green blob dissolving your unwanted slug-butter sandwich.

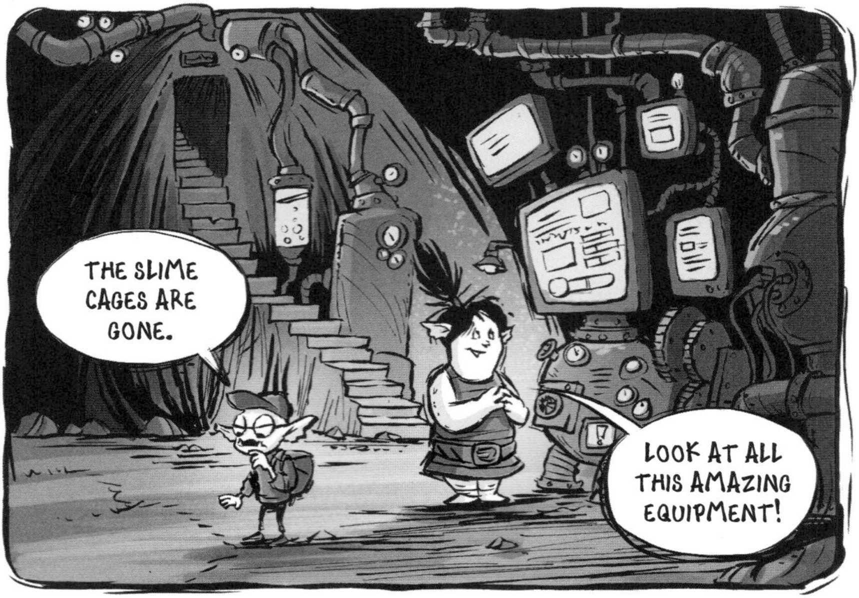
THE SLIME CAGES ARE GONE.
LOOK AT ALL THIS AMAZING EQUIPMENT!

A dim light glowed inside Mr. Snag's office. Gloomy shadows filled the room.

"Mr. Zallin?" I called out, but there was no answer.

"Maybe he's not here," Tank said.

"I'm glad I keep you around," I said. That earned me a slap on the head.

We crept into the room. It was a mess of open boxes waiting to be unpacked and tools waiting to be organized. In one corner sat a pile of Mr. Snag's things. Books on caring for slimes, and red coveralls with the Guild of Cleaners crest, all tossed to one side. Just like Mr. Snag.

Against the far wall stood a set of tall shelves packed with boxes, cables, wires and tools. But there was no sign of Zal.

The shelf against the far wall shuddered. Fine dust drifted to the floor.

"What was that?" Tank hissed.

"Weaver's spies?" I said. I didn't believe it though. Mr. Snag didn't like Weaver's spider babies scurrying around down here. He kept the place cobweb free so they'd have no place to hide. Whatever shook the shelf, it wasn't a spider.

The shelf trembled again. Dust rained down from the shelves. It glittered in the dim light and drew me closer.

"What are you doing?" Tank whispered, one foot out the doorway.

I peered into the darkness behind the boxes on the shelf.

"Fizz, be careful!" Tank hissed.

At that moment, I was more curious than scared. Something was moving behind this shelf. I pulled on the shelf, but it didn't budge.

"It must be screwed to the wall," I said.

"Um, Fizz." Tank's eyes went wide. The blood drained from her warty green skin. "Look at your hands."

My hands and clothes were covered in dust. That's to be expected when you go rummaging around boxes in the school basement.

"Relax, Tank," I said to my worried friend. "I'll wash my hands before lunch."

"You'd better not!" she snapped. "Take a closer look at the stuff."

I stepped into the light near the door and examined the dust. Immediately I wished I had stayed in the dark.

Purple dust covered my fingers. The dust glittered and popped, like it was alive.

Purple dust covered the floor in front of the shelf and many of the boxes in the small room. This much magic in one place could get the school shut down for a long time. Our mystery had just gotten magical. For a goblin detective, that is not a good thing.

CHAPTER NINE
Shadows and Strangers

The Shadow Tower loomed over us like an angry gym teacher.

"Coming here was a bad idea," I said.

"Tell me something I don't know," Tank snapped. "But it's the only place Aleetha could meet us."

The thick obsidian walls of the School of Shadows circled the tall tower. Each stone was a perfectly carved square and darker than the bottom of Fang Harbor. Being so close to all this magic sent my tail twitching.

Tank wasn't happy either. Her hair had been standing on end since we trekked up here from school.

"This place radiates magic," she said. "My phone is going haywire."

"I'm surprised you got a message to Aleetha," I said. "I thought mages couldn't use technology."

Tank's warty face split into a wide grin.

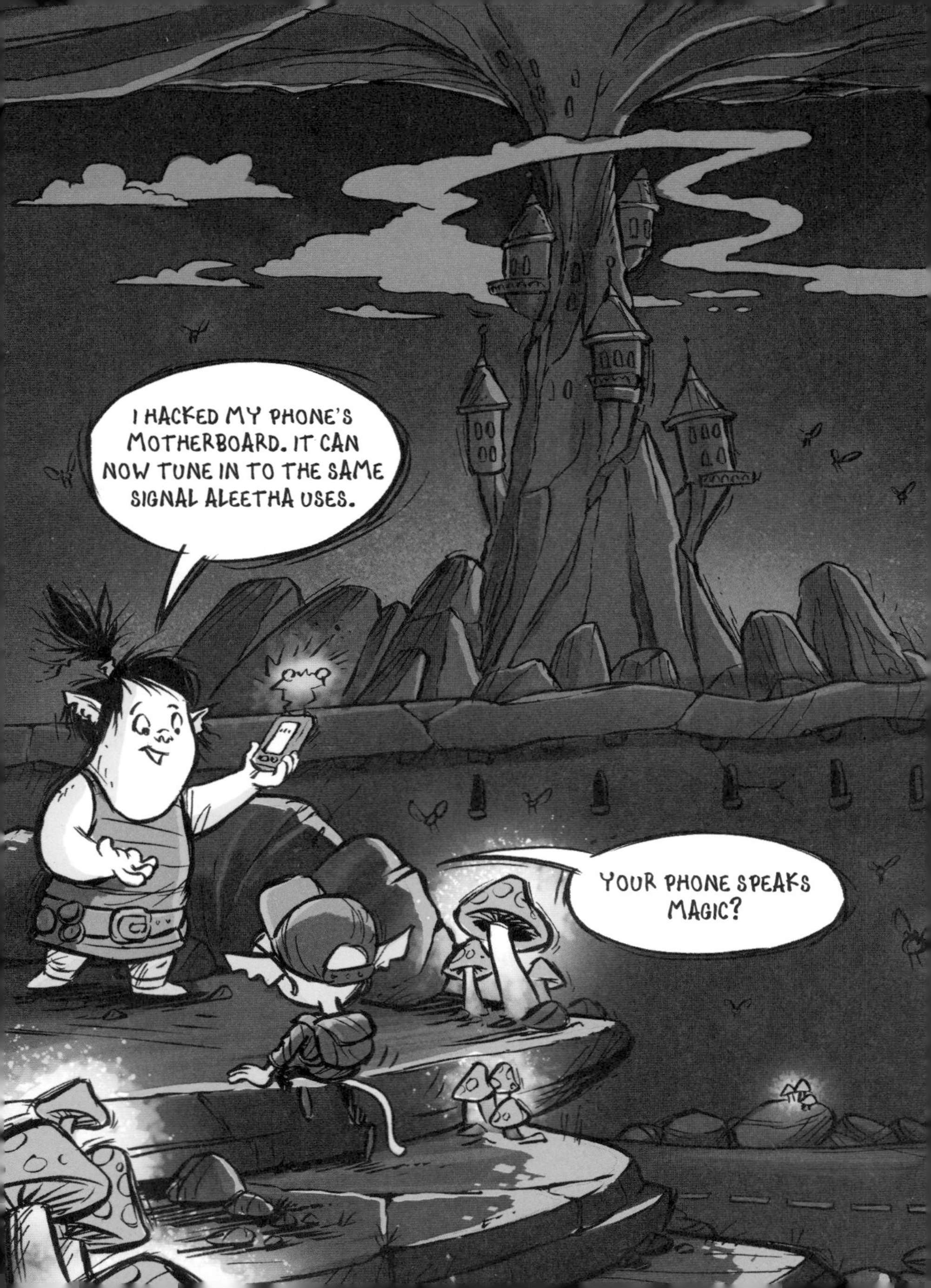
I HACKED MY PHONE'S MOTHERBOARD. IT CAN NOW TUNE IN TO THE SAME SIGNAL ALEETHA USES.
YOUR PHONE SPEAKS MAGIC?

"Sort of," Tank said with a modest shrug of her shoulders. "It's a work in progress. Right now, we can send short messages to each other. Being this close to so much magic is sending the protocol receivers into overload."

"Naturally," I said. When Tank gets talking technical, it's easier to just pretend you know what she's talking about.

At that moment, I was more concerned with how long this was taking. The light from the glowshrooms lining the path back into town was growing dim. It would be night soon. If I wasn't home by the time the glowshrooms went dark, Mom would freak. A freaking mom is never a good thing.

The Shadow Tower stretched upward, reaching the rock ceiling high above Slick City. Made of a single solid chunk of obsidian, the Shadow Tower had been a gift from the Mages of the Spire long ago when the first deposits of the black liquid known as slick were discovered below Fang Harbor. The mages knew the small village would grow to be the city it is today. As more and more machines were powered by slick instead of magic, many monsters thought the mages would go away. They did not. Over the years, a school of wizardry was built around the Shadow Tower. The dark mages within rarely ventured outside the tower. And that was just fine with the monsters of Slick City.

From goblins to ogres and everything in between, monsters and magic did not get along. As a rule, monsters did not mess with magic. That way, magic did not mess with them. Why bother with the dangers of magic— getting blown up, turned into a toad and all that other nasty stuff—when you could just use technology? Good old slick-powered tech never failed. Okay, hardly ever failed. But at least you didn't get banished to the Dark Depths because you pressed the wrong button on the TV remote.

The wall at the base of the Shadow Tower shimmered yellow to form a small doorway. A dark shape stepped out from the glow.

"Aleetha!" Tank dashed to the lava elf and hugged her so hard that she lifted her off the ground.

"Great to see you too, Tank!" Aleetha said, struggling to breathe under the troll's grip. "Try not to break anything."

Tank let her down with a thud.

We hadn't seen each other since the start of school. Aleetha had grown taller. She now wore the purple robes of a student of magic. It suited her fiery-orange skin and black hair. I could hardly believe that just last year she was in our class at Gravelmuck Elementary. At the end of the year, she went for her magic exams at the School of Shadows and passed them all. She was accepted with full honors and now spent her days and nights inside the university, learning to be a mage under the watchful gaze of the Shadow Tower and the wizards within.

Personally, I'd rather pick skunk shells in the Tar Wastes north of the city than learn magic. But whatever waggles your tail, right?

"I don't have much time," Aleetha said. "My enchantment class is starting soon."

"School in the evening?" Tank said.

Aleetha smiled. "No rest for us wizards."

When she finished school, Aleetha would be licensed to practice magic. Considering what we had found in Mr. Snag's office, she was the perfect person to answer our question.

"Go on," Tank said to me. "Show her."

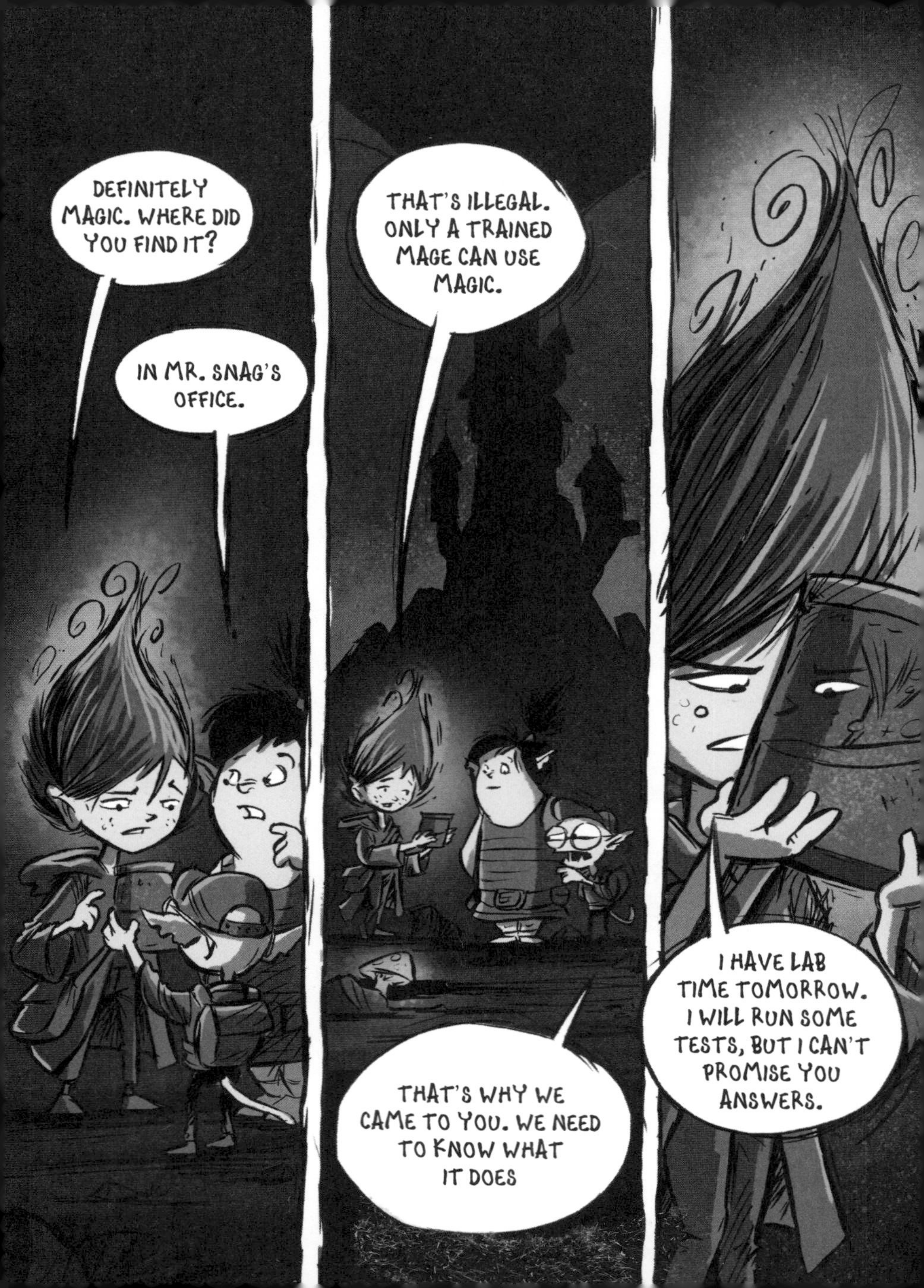

DEFINITELY MAGIC. WHERE DID YOU FIND IT?
IN MR. SNAG'S OFFICE.
THAT'S ILLEGAL. ONLY A TRAINED MAGE CAN USE MAGIC.
THAT'S WHY WE CAME TO YOU. WE NEED TO KNOW WHAT IT DOES
I HAVE LAB TIME TOMORROW. I WILL RUN SOME TESTS, BUT I CAN'T PROMISE YOU ANSWERS.

"Even the chance of some answers is better than nothing," Tank said. "Thanks, Aleetha."

The elf smiled. "Anything for my old detective partners." The wall behind us shimmered yellow again.

"That's my signal," Aleetha said. "I better not be late for class. Detention around here is not fun. Trust me."

I shivered at the thought of being at the mercy of a teacher with magic powers.

Aleetha moved back to the glowing doorway she'd come through. She held up the jar of purple dust. "I'll message you with the results, Tank."

She stepped into the yellow light and vanished. The wall became dark again. It was like she had never been there.

The glowshrooms were nearly out. Hanging around a wizard school at night was not my idea of a good time, so I got my tail away from there as quickly as I could.

We walked in silence, but my brain rang loudly with questions. Who would use magic at our school? What did that strange dust do? Why was that garbage truck following us?

"Tank," I said under my breath, "when is garbage pick-up day?"

Behind us, a large garbage truck rumbled around the corner and stopped in the middle of the quiet street.

"Not until next week. Why?"

I glanced over my shoulder. The truck was close to us. A big, filthy, grumbling, smoke-spewing mass of machinery. I could see inside the front window. A hairy ogre sat in the driver's seat. Staring at us.

"I have a feeling we're next on the pick-up schedule."

The garbage truck roared to life. It charged down the street toward us.

CHAPTER TEN
Weekend and Writers

*C*lack, clack, clack.

Someone was hammering in my brain.

Clack, clack, clack.

That someone was my mom. But it wasn't a hammer. It was a computer. All that clacking was the sound of inspiration. Mom was writing. I pictured her in the other room, staring at the computer screen, completely focused on her article for the newspaper.

My detective brain went through the facts.

Fact #1
Mom is home working.
Fact #2
I'm still in bed.
WEEKEND!

And the weekend meant no school. Is there anything better than waking up to a day with no school?

I pulled the covers back over my head. Time for more shut-eye. Detectives need a lot of sleep. But those runaway slimes were running laps around my brain.

Whoever released the slimes had a key to the front door of the school. They knew where to find the slimes and how to lead them outside. Mr. Snag had both the key and the skill to lead slimes. I just couldn't see him putting his beasts in that much danger. Where were the slimes? No one could answer that question either. The poor things were probably starving. I hoped that wherever they were, they had some dirt to chew on.

And what was with Principal Weaver hauling us into her office? We didn't do anything wrong. And now she was all buddy-buddy with Mr. Zallin, the new caretaker with the cleaning machines. Weaver's sticky webs were wrapped up in this mystery somehow.

Which left me wondering about the deranged garbage ogre from the night before. We had managed to outrun him, but I had a feeling we hadn't seen the last of Mr. Ugly and his garbage truck. Who in the name of Rockfall Mountain was he? And why did he chase us?

This mystery had more questions than one of Mr. Mantle's pop quizzes.

My stomach grumbled, telling my brain to stop working so hard. I took its advice and stumbled into the kitchen to get some breakfast.

Mom didn't look up from her computer when I walked in. I figured she must be on a roll with the writing. I poured a bowl of Crunchy Critter cereal and plopped down beside her on the couch. She had her feet up on the coffee table, computer in her lap and mug of coffee steaming beside her. Full-on writer mode.

"Did you know," she announced without even taking her eyes from her computer screen, "that the Gremlin Gang has robbed six art galleries, museums and antique shops in the last six months?"

"They have good taste," I said, crunching sugary critters in my mouth.

"They use their magic to get into banks and galleries," she said.

"I thought only elves used magic."

"Elves and demons from the Dark Depths, way down deep under the mountain. Apparently, gremlins are minor demons. They can perform lesser magic.

Break machines, open locks, that type of thing. They're ugly-looking too."

"That is Snatch Monsoon, the Gremlin Gang leader and a master of disguise. He's wanted in five cities across Rockfall Mountain." Mom paused to sip her coffee. "Last month, Snatch disguised himself as the owner of an art gallery in Lava Hills, not far from Slick City. He walked into the gallery and told the employees to pack all the paintings into the back of his truck. The real owner showed up an hour later to an empty gallery and a very confused group of employees."

"Gremlins get points for being creative," I said.

"My sources at the police station say Slick City is their next stop," Mom said.

"But gremlins can't be near water, and Slick City has Fang Harbor."

"True. Slick City is normally gremlin-free, but all the police in town are on the lookout for them." Mom flipped through the research notes scattered on the couch beside her. She let out a long sigh. "If only I could figure out what disguise they're using before they strike again. Exposing the Gremlin Gang would make this story a real winner."

"All your stories are winners, Mom," I said. Hey, it pays to lay it on thick with your mom every now and then.

"You're sweet, kid." Mom tickled the scales on my neck. "But you're still cleaning your room this weekend."

Dang. Can't blame a goblin for trying.

Mom put down her coffee and started typing again. That signaled we were done talking.

Fine by me. I'd finished my cereal. And I had my own investigation to dive into. But first, I had a troll to talk to.

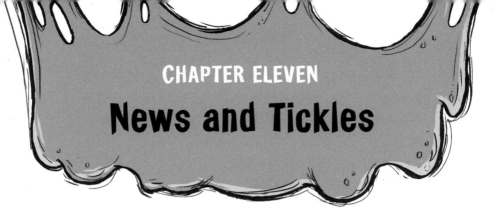

CHAPTER ELEVEN
News and Tickles

Tank pulled me through her front door. "You're just in time."

Her home was small and crowded. That's what you get when you put ten trolls into one cave. Mothers, fathers, sisters, brothers and grandparents, and all the noise and love that comes with them. Going over to Tank's place was like going to a party. There was always food cooking, music playing and laughter bouncing off the walls. It made my little apartment with just me and my mom seem so quiet and small. But quiet and small has its good parts too. I'm not complaining.

Two tiny trolls, barely out of diapers, burst from behind the couch. They danced around us in the narrow corridor.

"Fizz is here! Fizz is here!"

"Away with you, girls!" Tank said, waving her arms. She snarled playfully at the girls. They screamed and ran into the crowded kitchen, giggling.

"Dreena and Draana are getting big," I said.

"Big pain in the butt." Tank opened a small door carved into the stone wall at the end of the hallway. "Come on, let's get downstairs before my mom sees you."

"Fizz Marlow!" a voice thundered from the kitchen. "Is my favorite little goblin here?"

Tank sighed. "Too late."

Mrs. Wrenchlin came into the hall, wiping her glasses on her shirt. She put them on her large warty face and peered down at me.

"Why yes, it is Fizz!" She smiled. "Girls, you were right! We have a guest."

Dreena and Draana popped their heads out from behind Mrs. Wrenchlin's legs. They stuck their tongues out at Tank and disappeared again, still giggling.

"We were just going to the workshop, Mom," Tank said wearily. "We're working on a case. No time to talk or eat."

Tank pulled me down the stairs and into the workshop. The scent of home-cooked beetle brisket lingered in my snout.

The shop was an explosion of tools, wires and gadgetry. But it was an organized explosion. Shelves ran along the stone walls, lined with boxes and bins. Each box and bin had a neatly printed label that said *circuit boards, diodes, heat sinks, transformers* or some other tool of technology I did not understand. Tank did, and so did her mom.

This was their workshop. They had built it together and now spent many evenings tinkering, building and creating. Tank's mom was a tugboat captain, working the waters of Fang Harbor, so she normally worked with much bigger gears and circuits than these. This workshop was a place for her to pass on the love of engineering to her daughter. And it worked.

Tank picked something small off the workbench and held it out to me. It was a brass ball the size of a cave apple.

"Check this out!" she said. Her eyes gleamed with pride. "I call it the Ticklebot 1.0!"

I stepped away from the ball. "What does it do?" Getting too close to one of Tank's inventions was a great way to get covered in grime, toasted in flames or electrocuted. I had learned the hard way. Having a tinkering troll as a friend comes with some risks.

"A good question." She grinned. "Let's test it out on my sisters."

I looked around. "But they're upstairs."

"No, they're not," she said.

Tank marched out of the workshop and to a corner of the basement where a washing machine stood. She reached into a pile of laundry and pulled out two giggling trolls. Dreena and Draana.

"How'd they get down here?"

"With these two, it's always best to just assume they're spying on you." Tank carried the twins back into the workshop. She dropped them on the floor. They stood looking at us with wide eyes.

"We weren't spying!" Dreena screeched.

"Mom sent us down here!" Draana added.

"Whatever. Stand there," Tank ordered.

We stepped back from the girls.

WATCH THIS.

OH, SHINY!

PRETTY!

Tank ran to the Ticklebot. "Those arms were meant to tickle Dreena and Draana! Not you, Fizz. I'm sorry."

"Apologies later!" I wailed. "Make it stop!"

The arms had me pinned to the ground with their tickling. I couldn't move. All I could do was laugh. Having someone tickle you can be fun, but not if they don't stop when you ask them to. Tank's Ticklebot was definitely not stopping.

Tank pressed the Ticklebot. Inside the little ball, metal clicked against metal. The arms stopped their tickling. They zipped back into the tiny ball and disappeared. It was like they'd never been there.

I stumbled to my feet. My head swam from all that tickling. Dreena and Draana giggled like the Ticklebot had attacked them.

Tank carried the Ticklebot back to her workbench. "I have to work on the bot's targeting mechanisms."

"You have the whole tickling side of things perfected," I said. "I don't want to see another feather for as long as I live!"

"I wonder what went wrong," Tank mumbled. She put the bot back on her workbench. She opened a small hatch on the little bot's side and poked at the colored wires with a narrow screwdriver. "I have to get to the bottom of this. Won't take long."

When Tank is working on one of her creations, "won't take long" means "get comfortable—this is going to be awhile."

I switched on the TV on the wall above the workbench. I immediately wished I hadn't.

"Mr. Trellik!" I said.

"What's he doing talking to Trina Trallastar on TV?"

Onscreen, the owner of the antiques store was talking excitedly to the SlickTV news reporter. It looked like he had a worm in his ear. I turned up the volume.

"Tell us more about Firebane's Hoard, Mr. Trellik," Trina said in her sweetest TV voice.

Mr. Trellik smiled nervously. "Firebane's Hoard is a collection of the finest treasures from the vaults of the master of the Dark Depths himself, Firebane Drakeclaw. The treasures are touring Rockfall Mountain and will be on display at Trellik's Treasures all this week."

"Sounds exciting!" Trina gushed. "Back to you in the newsroom!"

The camera jumped back to the anchor at her desk. She started talking about the weather.

"No wonder old Trellik freaked out about the slimes on his steps!" Tank said.

"Firebane's Hoard will bring a lot of visitors to his shop this week," I said. "That dragon is ancient! He's been hoarding treasure since Rockfall Mountain was a hill. I bet he's got some cool stuff."

COOL AND EXPENSIVE.

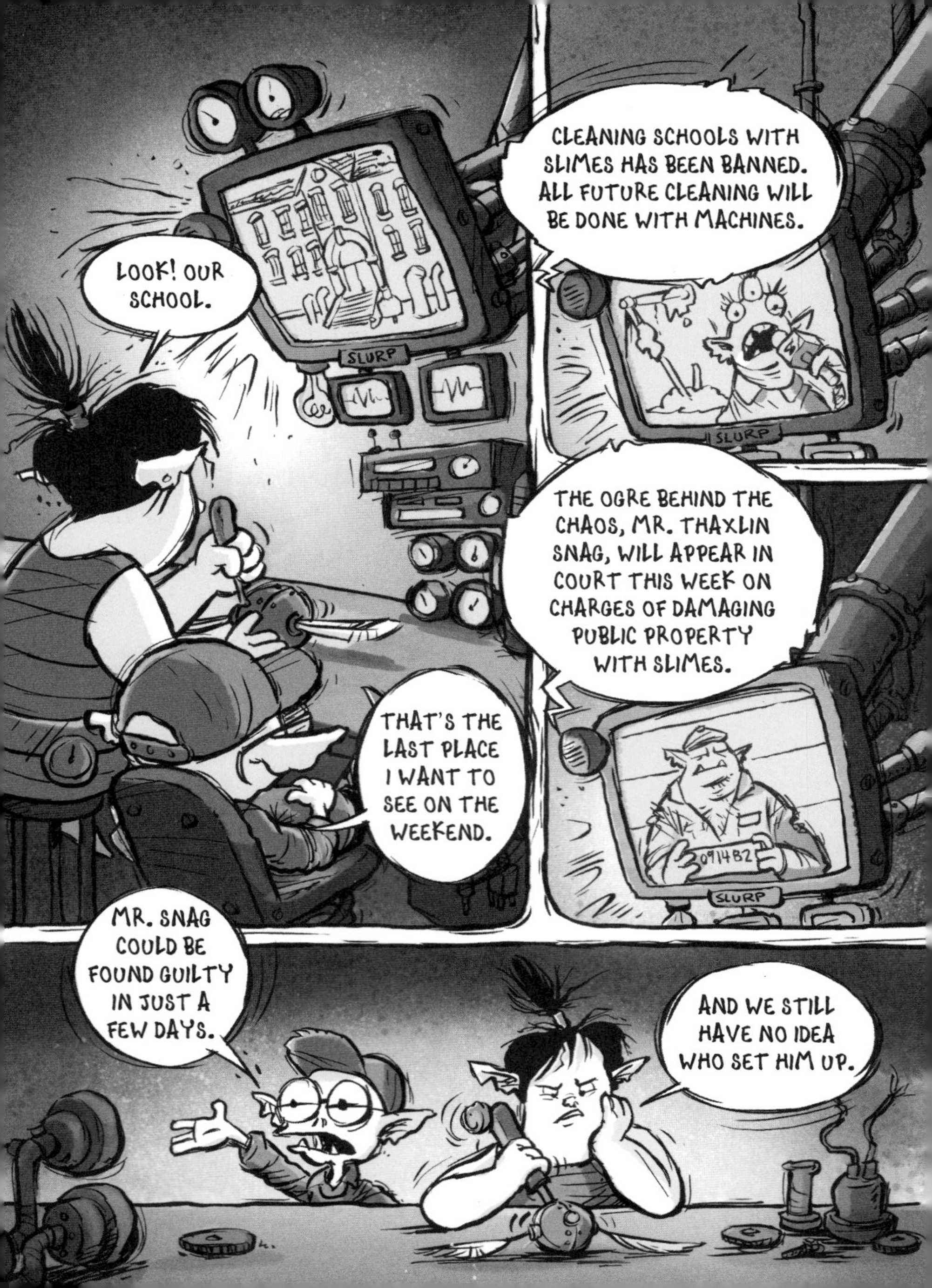
LOOK! OUR SCHOOL.
CLEANING SCHOOLS WITH SLIMES HAS BEEN BANNED. ALL FUTURE CLEANING WILL BE DONE WITH MACHINES.
SLURP
SLURP
THE OGRE BEHIND THE CHAOS, MR. THAXLIN SNAG, WILL APPEAR IN COURT THIS WEEK ON CHARGES OF DAMAGING PUBLIC PROPERTY WITH SLIMES.
THAT'S THE LAST PLACE I WANT TO SEE ON THE WEEKEND.
0914B2
SLURP
MR. SNAG COULD BE FOUND GUILTY IN JUST A FEW DAYS.
AND WE STILL HAVE NO IDEA WHO SET HIM UP.

CHAPTER TWELVE
Bullies and Balls

The rest of the weekend should have been filled with homework, but my mind was stuck on Mr. Snag and those slimes. The old ogre was as gentle as a granite sloth. There was no way he let the slimes loose. I didn't have much to go on, but I just knew Snag was set up. My hunch didn't make much difference though. By the start of the week, Tank and I still didn't know what to do. And I still didn't have my homework done.

To make things worse, we had gym class.

I don't know who invented this part of our curriculum, but they should be dropped into the fire pit of the Howling Suck. I know, I know. Gym is great! Gym is fun! You get to run around. You get to scream. All good in theory. But when you have Rizzo Rawlins in your class and a gang of goons to back him up, gym becomes forty minutes of bangs, bumps and bruises.

Even when I'm on the same team as Rizzo and the ogre twins, they still manage to bash, bang and bloody me.

Whoever invented dodgeball should be tossed into that fire pit too.

"Don't sweat it, Fizz," Tank said when I sat on the bench beside her. "Rizzo is just excited because his dad is taking them all on vacation next month."

"Vacation? In the middle of the school year?"

"Yeah, he was bragging about it at lunch. His dad's business is doing really well. Some big deal or something."

The walls of the gym trembled.

"Here we go again," Tank said. "Grab hold of something."

The entire gym shook, sending kids falling to the ground. As soon as it came, the shaking stopped.

"It's just the heater," Ms. Blinx barked. "Get back into the game!"

"That's the third tremor today," Tank said. "They're happening more often. Hope Mr. Zallin fixes the heater soon."

"What exactly is wrong with the heater?" I put my hand over the heating vent behind our bench. "It's not cold in here. And there's hot air coming out of this vent."

Tank wasn't listening. She was on her feet, walking to the equipment room. I followed her.

"What is that doing here?" she said. She ran her finger through a pile of purple dust on the ground outside the door. "Interesting."

She opened the door to the equipment room.

It was packed with balls, sticks, nets and other gym equipment. A line of purple dust trailed into the small room and disappeared behind a ball hockey net.

Tank stepped into the room. She pointed her camera at the trail and took a photo. I leaned down to get a closer look at the dust.

"It's the same stuff as in Zal's office," I said.

The trail disappeared under an old hockey net. I tugged on it to get it out of the way. It wouldn't move. But it did growl.

The little creature bounced around the room, screeching like I had stuck it with a knife. Hockey sticks clattered to the ground. Its sharp claws burst soccer balls and ripped crash mats as it jumped from wall to wall. All I saw was its tiny blue body scrambling into the heating vent.

Then the room was silent except for Tank's heavy breathing beside me.

"What was that?" I said.

"I have no idea."

The door to the equipment room flew open.

The whole class stood in the doorway. Dodgeball game forgotten. Rizzo Rawlins stood at the front of the pack.

"Figures the detective duds would trash the place," he howled. "Just like their caretaker pal trashed the schoolyard!"

That got the whole class laughing. Ms. Blinx buzzed around behind them, telling them to stop and get back to the game. The kids drifted away, but the laughter didn't stop. And our trouble wasn't over.

A dark shadow fell over the doorway. Mr. Zallin's large body blocked the light from the gym.

"Look at what you have done!" His deep voice boomed. His eyes blazed red. His whole face scowled. I'd never seen a caretaker so mad before. "You have destroyed school property! Principal Weaver will hear of this."

In the caretaker's face, I saw more than just anger. I saw something familiar. I just couldn't place it.

As he marched us down to Principal Weaver's office, I knew I had more to worry about than an angry caretaker. We'd just seen a creature that didn't belong in our school. Something dark was happening here. I was determined to find out what. But first, I had an angry principal to face.

CHAPTER THIRTEEN
Purple Goes Pow

Fang Harbor is always a busy place. Weekdays after school are no exception.

Every minute of every day, ships loaded with cargo sail in and out of the large underground port. Nestled in the safety of a giant cave, Fang Harbor has only one exit to the outside world—the Mouth. The top of the wide cave opening on the far side of the water is lined with jagged javelins of rock. These sharp rocks look like teeth and are what gave the harbor its name.

Beyond the Mouth lie the open sea and the surface world. I've always wanted to know more about the monsters living outside the mountain. But there are enough mysteries under this rock to keep me busy for now.

All around me, trucks, cranes and armies of dock workers scrambled to unload crates packed with fruits, vegetables, furniture, toys and anything else needed inside the mountain. Dozens of container ships would arrive that day, fully loaded. They'd drop their cargo and sail out, hauling minerals, mushrooms, barrels of valuable slick and other treasures the mountain had to offer.

Tank and I sat under the statue of Tiberious the Brave, the founding ogre of Slick City. He didn't actually *find* the place. We goblins lived along these beaches for centuries before Tiberious showed up. The ogres won't tell you that part of the story. They like to take all the credit themselves. There aren't any statues for the goblin tribesmen who showed Tiberious how to turn slick into fuel. But goblins used the goopy black stuff under the sand to light their lamps for years before the ogres came along and pumped it out of the ground. Now the stuff keeps the entire Rockfall Mountain running. From gadgets to cars, slick is the stuff that makes it happen. And goblins were the first to use it. You won't have much luck finding that in Mr. Mantle's history books.

But then there's Mr. Snag. He's an ogre, and I'm working to prove he's innocent.

Old Tiberious's hairy stone feet made a good spot to sit and wait. We weren't alone. A pair of teenage goblins sat against the statue's other leg. They had their heads together, sharing a pair of headphones. They bopped their heads like yo-yos to some song I couldn't hear.

Teenagers. Who gets them? Not this detective.

For me, the best part of the harbor was the monster-watching. I'd sit with my notebook and create stories about the monsters who passed by. Tank loved watching the ships chug their way slowly through the murky water. She had seawater in her bones, just like the rest of her family.

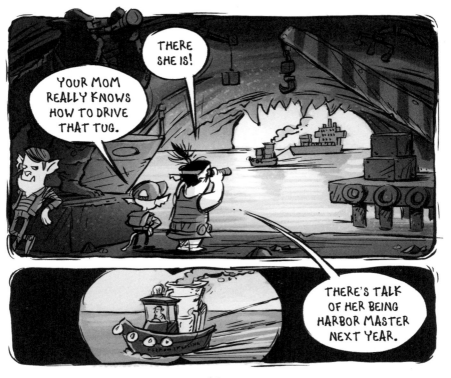

I wasn't the only one unimpressed by Aleetha's sudden appearance. The goblin teens gave her a wary look and moved to the far side of the harbor. Aleetha's purple robes stood out against the brown rocks around us. Only students from the Shadow Tower wore robes of that color. Passing monsters crossed to the far side of the harbor path as they neared us. No one wanted to get close to the mysterious elf or her magic. Maybe arranging to meet Aleetha in public wasn't such a good idea.

"Sorry for startling you. It's just so much fun scaring the brave detectives of Gravelmuck Elementary." Aleetha's eyes twinkled. She wasn't bothered by the stares from other monsters. Maybe they taught her that at mage school.

"We don't have time for games," I grumbled. "Mr. Snag is going to court tomorrow. The judge will decide if he's responsible for letting the slimes out and damaging the school."

"And you don't think he is?" Aleetha said.

"It just doesn't add up," Tank said. "Mr. Snag loved his job and he loved his slimes. There's no reason why he would let them do all that damage."

"And there's all that weird stuff happening at our school," I said.

"What weird stuff?"

"This weird stuff." Tank handed her camera to Aleetha.

The elf's brow furrowed as she watched Tank's video from the equipment room.

It was a mess of red eyes, blue skin and flying soccer balls. You couldn't make out what the creature looked like, but it did prove that we hadn't caused all the damage. When we showed the video to Principal Weaver, it saved us from a year's worth of detention. She didn't seem too concerned that there were mysterious red-eyed creatures hiding in the equipment room. Who knows what goes on in the mind of a principal?

"Hard to say what that thing is," Aleetha said when she finished watching the video. She handed the camera back to Tank. "It's moving so quickly, and all we see are its shadows. Could be an imp."

Tank moaned. "Oh, no, not imps! Our neighbor's cave was infested with those little critters last summer. It was a mess."

"They get everywhere," Aleetha said. "They chew through wires, burst pipes and much worse."

"Yeah, but would they cause the whole school to shake?" I said.

"No, but this stuff could." Aleetha held up a small ball of soft putty.

"Is that play putty?" Tank asked. "The twins love that stuff."

"Then they would really like this." Aleetha walked toward a set of stairs that led to the water. "Follow me."

She stopped at a quiet spot on the beach.

She pushed her thumb into the putty to make a hole. "Hold this."

She handed me the putty ball and pulled a little cloth pouch from her bag. She poured the purple powder into the tiny hole.

"Watch what happens when we add that purple powder you found."

Aleetha took the putty ball back. She closed up the hole so that the powder was completely covered. Then she put the ball on the sand near the water.

She grinned as she walked back to us. "Ready?"

"Are you going to turn it into an imp?" I asked.

"No, but I'm tempted to turn you into one."

I stopped with the lame jokes. It's never good to make a wizard angry. Even a wizard-in-training.

"Watch."

She stared at the ball. In a quiet voice, she said words in a language no monster outside of the Shadow Tower would understand.

"The purple powder is an explosive," I said.

"But there was no sound," Tank said. She moved to where the ball had been only a moment before. Now there was a crater in the sand. "No pop or bang or anything. It was completely quiet."

"Exactly." Aleetha grinned. "I played with it in the lab at school. It's an explosive that's been filled with magic to take away all the noise."

"Perfect for blowing stuff up without anyone noticing," Tank said.

She was right. Around us, the harbor continued to bustle with activity. Trolls and ogres sauntered along the docks. Boats moved around the piers. It was as if nothing had happened.

"Why blow something up if you can't make it go boom?" I said. "The noise is the best part."

"You'll have to ask the monsters using this powder."

"Monsters can't use magic," I said.

"Monsters that live up here near the surface can't use magic," Aleetha said. "But there are beasts from the Dark Depths that can tap into the forces of magic."

"We found the powder in our school." Tank tugged her spiky hair with worry. "That means somebody at Gravelmuck is messing with monsters from the Depths?"

"Another reason for you two to drop this case." Aleetha looked hard at both of us. "Trust me, you do not want to mess with creatures from that deep under the mountain."

The air behind her shimmered with a yellow glow.

"Time to go. I'm late for my transmutation class." Aleetha stepped into the yellow light. She turned to us. The teasing was gone from her voice. "Be very careful with this one. Okay?"

She stepped into the glowing doorway and vanished.

We didn't say much on the walk home. Both of us were deep in our own thoughts. I couldn't shake the feeling that this mystery was growing too big for a pair of fourth-grade detectives.

Who at our school would have contact with monsters from the Dark Depths? That realm was serious business. The Depths was not a place you went on summer vacation. Demons and dragons lived down there. Any monster with half a tail knew not to mess with monsters from the Depths. And now someone at Gravelmuck Elementary was doing just that.

And what was the deal with the magic powder? It made things go boom without any noise. Why would anyone need that at our school? What did it have to do with the escaped slimes? More questions to add to the pile cluttering up my brain.

Don't get me wrong—I like questions. It's what keeps me in the detective game. But every once in a while, a case comes along that pushes even my limits. Where were the slimes? Did Principal Weaver let them escape so she could get rid of Mr. Snag? Why was a garbage truck racing straight for us again?

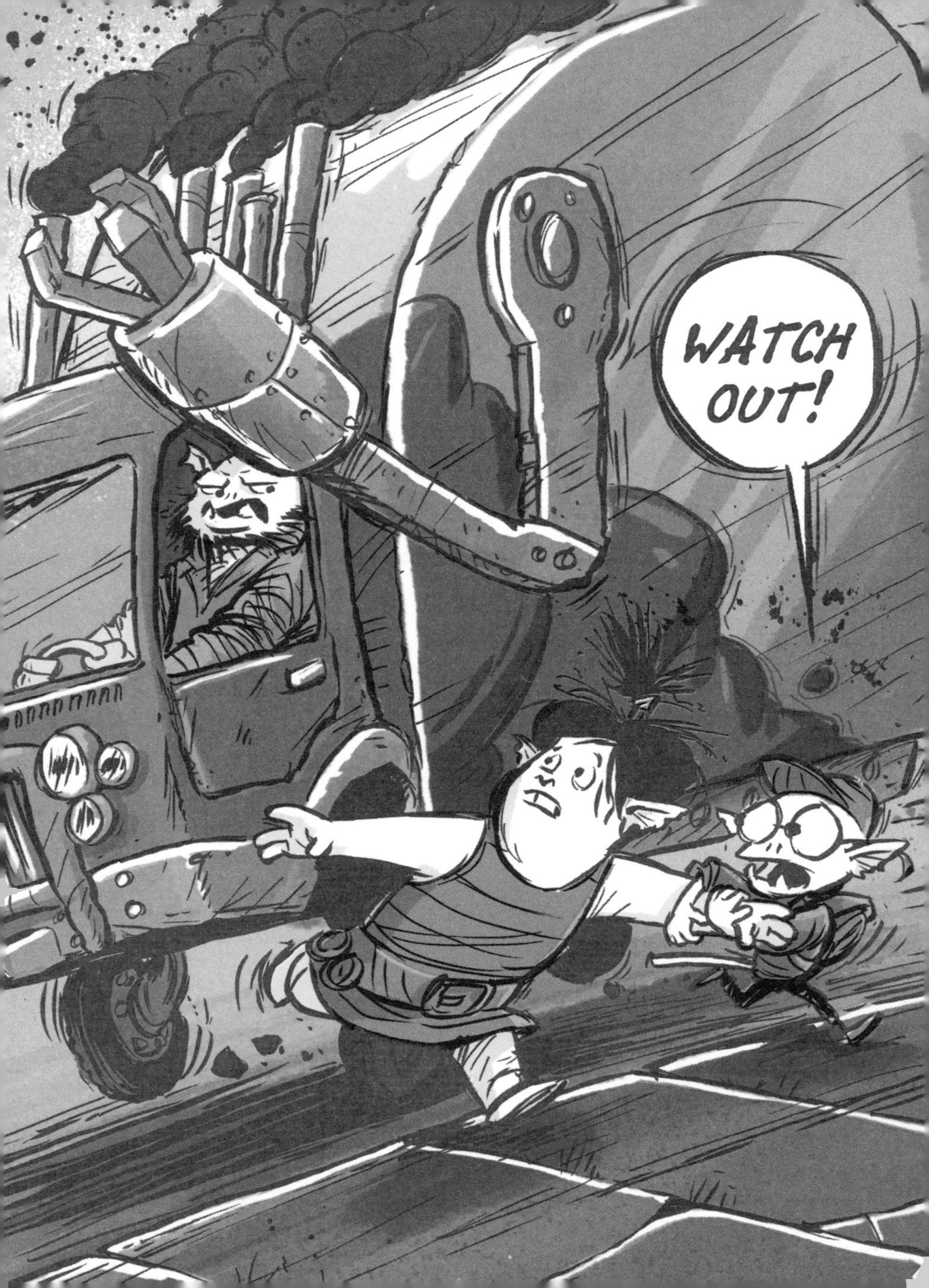
WATCH OUT!

The truck screeched to a stop right where we had been standing only a second before. Angry black smoke billowed from the exhaust pipe. In the dump tanks in the back, two large slimes fell off the pile of garbage they had been devouring.

The driver's door opened. A pair of heavy boots emerged, followed by a pair of very large legs attached to a wide chest and hairy face that looked familiar.

"Oh no," Tank said. She scrambled to her feet. "It's the ogre from the Shadow Tower!"

The ogre's dark eyes locked onto us. His thick eyebrows scrunched together.

"There you are," he said in a growly voice. He rolled up his sleeves, like he was getting ready to toss us into the back of his garbage truck.

"And here we go!" Tank yelped and ran down the street.

I took the hint and followed her. The ogre also got the hint and followed me.

"Get back here!" he boomed. He lumbered down the road behind us. Running wasn't something this guy did a lot. It took him a few steps to gain some speed. But when he did, his extra weight gave him momentum.

I could hear his heavy footsteps pounding closer with every step.

Tank took a sharp turn into a dark alley between two tall buildings. I was right behind her. I ran down the alley.

And into a wall.

It was a dead end. Some bright monster had decided to block the alley with a very strong, very steep wall. Boxes and garbage bags lined the walls, but there were no doors, ladders or anything else of use to a goblin about to be crushed by an angry ogre. And there was also no Tank.

Panic welled up inside me. Tank had ditched me. She had left me behind to save her own troll skin.

"So this is how it ends," I said to the bags of garbage. "Abandoned by my friend and left to be smushed by an angry garbage ogre."

"There you are!"

The very large, very angry shape of the ogre filled the open end of the alley. I closed my eyes and waited for the smushing to begin.

CHAPTER FOURTEEN
Ticklebot 2.0

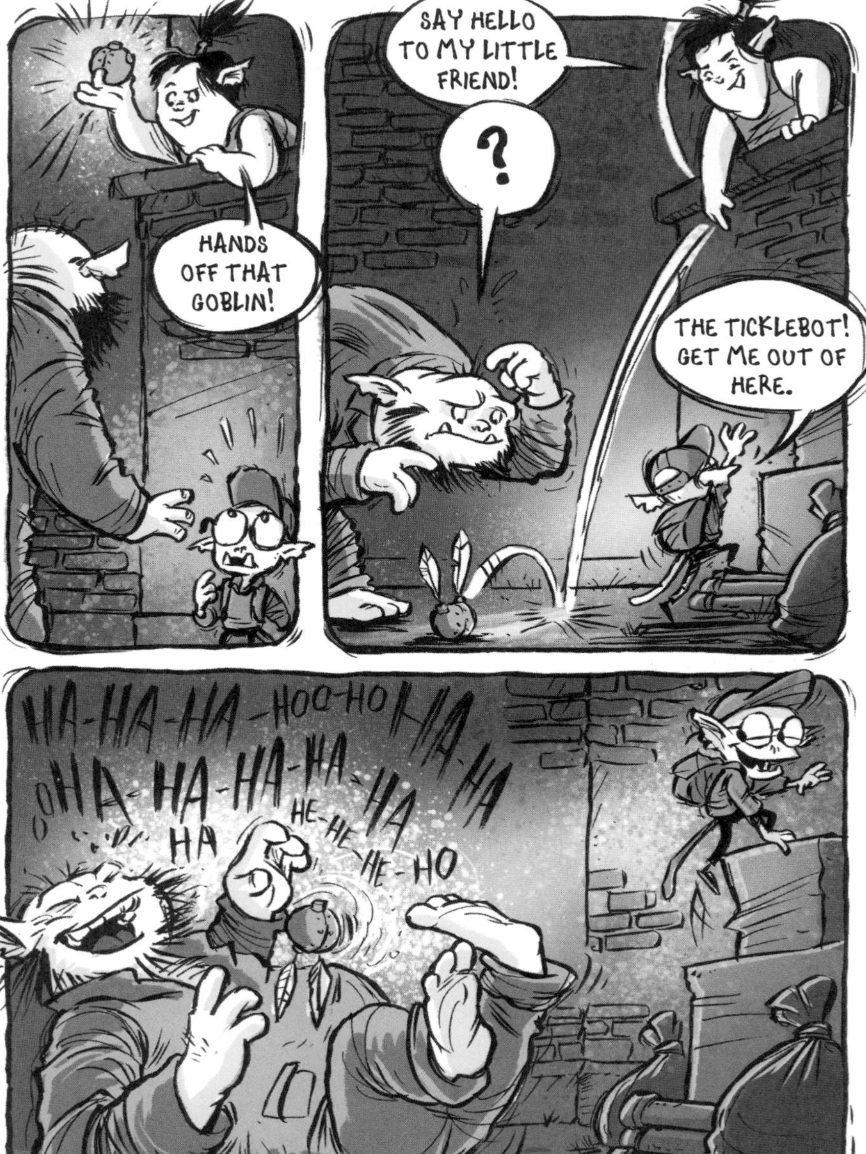
HANDS OFF THAT GOBLIN!
SAY HELLO TO MY LITTLE FRIEND!
?
THE TICKLEBOT! GET ME OUT OF HERE.
HA-HA-HA-HOO-HO HA-HA-HA
HA-HA-HA-HA-HA-HA-HA
HA
HE-HE-HE-HO

The ogre didn't stand a chance. The Ticklebot's tentacles went for his soft spots. They zeroed in on that tender spot under every monster's chin. They tickled behind his knees. They tickled under his big armpits. He rolled around on the ground, howling with laughter.

Tank's Ticklebot had claimed another victim.

"Stop!" the ogre gasped between guffaws. He swatted away tentacles with his big beefy hands. But there were too many nimble ticklers for the big beast.

The Ticklebot had only just begun. If it was fully cranked, those tentacles would keep the ogre occupied long enough for us to escape.

"Move it, Fizz!" Tank shouted from the top of the wall. She reached down to pull me up.

"Stop! Stop!" the ogre pleaded. I was halfway up the wall when his words changed. "Snag! Snag!"

I let go of Tank's hand and dropped back to the ground.

Tank scowled. "Fizz! Get back up here. That thing won't keep him busy much longer."

I ignored her and raced to the helpless ogre. Tears of laughter streamed down his cheeks and soaked the bristles on his green face.

"What did you say?"

"Snag! Snag." He was going to say more but was lost to another fit of laughter as a tentacle caught the soft spot under his chin.

I called to Tank, "How do I stop this thing?"

"You don't," she barked from her perch on the top of the wall. "Fizz, we have to go. That ogre wants to feed us to his slimes!"

Dodging a pair of waving tentacles, I searched the brass ball. I'd seen Tank switch it off in her workshop. There was a button or switch or something. My fingers ran across a small raised square on the Ticklebot's surface. I pushed it.

Immediately, the tentacles went stiff, like icicles. They zipped back into the ball one at time with loud pops, until all that was left was a simple brass ball.

And a wheezing ogre.

I took a step back from the monster. He struggled to catch his breath from all that laughing. I hoped I hadn't just made a big mistake. He sat up and wiped a tear from his eye.

"Thank…you," he said. His chest heaved as he tried to speak.

"Do you know Mr. Snag?" I asked. "You said his name."

The ogre nodded slowly. He pulled a piece of paper from his pocket. He reached out with his large hairy hand and offered it to me.

"Read it," he said between heavy breaths.

Tank scrambled down from the wall. I opened the paper.

"You *do* know Mr. Snag!" Tank said.

Hutch got to his feet. "We joined the Guild of Cleaners together many years ago. We were just kids then, not much older than you."

He pointed to the crest on his chest. Two mops crossed over a slime. The sign of the Guild of Cleaners. Mr. Snag had the same crest on his work shirts.

"Are you a school caretaker too?" I asked.

He shook his head. "No, I collect garbage around Slick City."

"That explains the truck," Tank said. "And the slimes in the back."

"Scrapper and Fetch are two of the finest garbage-eating slimes I've ever had the pleasure of working with." Hutch chuckled. His big brown eyes got misty at the mention of his slimes. "Those two can chew through a pile of trash faster than Mayor Grimlock can take a bribe. And now slimes like them all over this city are in trouble."

"Trouble? How?"

"Schools have outlawed slime cleaning. All because somebody released Snag's slimes. Now they're replacing all the slimes with fancy cleaning machines in every school in the city. The slimes have nowhere to go. They'll all dry up if they're not cleaning the schools. Caretakers everywhere are worried about what will happen to their cleaning beasts."

Tank sighed. "We're having enough trouble clearing Mr. Snag's name. We can't save a bunch of slimes too."

"Yes, we can." Hutch smiled. "If we can prove someone released the slimes, we will clear Snag's name.

And we will show slimes are harmless when handled by responsible members of the Guild of Cleaners."

"First we actually have to find the slimes," I said.

Hutch scratched the bristles on his chin and grinned. "That's easy," he said. "Scrapper knows where they are."

"Scrapper the slime knows where the other slimes are?"

"Of course he does," Hutch said. "Follow me and he'll tell you himself."

Hutch's garbage truck was still parked where he had left it, on the side of the road. The slimes were in their tanks, happily devouring a pile of garbage. Hutch opened the driver's-side door and pulled out three sets of strange-looking headphones. Each had a cord ending in a wide suction cup. He handed us each a set and then gave the glass tank a few gentle taps. The slimes stopped their munching and slurped toward Hutch.

"They're answering your call," Tank said, her eyes wide in amazement. "I didn't know that was possible."

"They respond to vibrations," Hutch said. He pressed each of the suction cups from the headphones against the side of the glass tank. "There's a lot folks don't know about slimes. Just because they have no bones and eat garbage doesn't mean they aren't smart."

The larger of the two slimes pressed its gooey body against the glass where the suction cup was stuck.

"That's Scrapper. He usually does the talking. Fetch is kind of shy." Hutch put on the headphones and spoke into a tiny microphone attached to the side. "Hey, Scrap. This is Tank and Fizz. Tell them what you told me about Snag's cleaners."

Our mountain is filled with all kinds of life, from silent glowing mushrooms growing on rocks to super-intelligent dragons deep down in the Depths. Some creatures are very smart and run things in the mountain. Other creatures are not much smarter than the rocks that make up the mountain. I'd never thought of slimes as being much smarter than a pebble. I was wrong.

Hutch gathered the headphones. "I've asked them many questions, but all they say is the slimes are under the school and they're hungry."

"The poor things," Tank said. She gazed sadly at the slimes in the tank. "Just because they're slimes doesn't mean they can be taken away and treated badly. We have to find them, Fizz."

"How?" I said. "We've been searching all week, Tank. How are we going to find the slimes in time to save Mr. Snag?"

"With this," Hutch said. The ogre held up a small glass container the size of a pop can. It was half full of green slime. "This is Scrapper. Well, part of him. Slimes can sense each other. This slime will glow brightly when you are close to Snag's slimes."

Tank's eyes lit up. "Like a slime radar." She took the cube from Hutch. "It's cute."

"Drop this little guy into Snag's slimes when you find them," Hutch said. "That will tell Scrapper where you are. And we'll come to help."

The entire success of saving our caretaker came down to following a slime in a cube. We were in big trouble.

CHAPTER FIFTEEN
Smuggling Slime

Bringing a metal-chewing slime to school is never a good idea. I was taking a big risk. And not just the risk of the cube cracking in my bag and the slime dissolving my homework. Actually, that wouldn't be so bad.

I was risking getting kicked out of school.

After the slime escape, slimes had been officially banned in all schools. Getting caught with one in my backpack would get me booted out of school faster than Rizzo Rawlins could snatch lunch money from a first-grader.

Finding the slimes was the key to solving this mystery and clearing Mr. Snag. And that meant taking some risks. It didn't mean Tank was happy about our secret package though.

She met me outside the cafeteria at lunchtime.

"Let's get this over with," she said, a grim look on her warty face. "We have until the end of lunch to sneak down to the basement and find the missing slimes."

We hurried to the basement stairs but froze at the top when we heard voices in the main office.

OUR CARETAKER IS VERY HAPPY WITH THE NEW VACUUM CLEANER FROM YOUR COMPANY, MR. RAWLINS.

I'M HAPPY TOO!

BUSINESS IS BOOMING. WITH THE BAN ON SLIMES, EVERY SCHOOL IN THE CITY HAS ORDERED NEW VACUUMS.

THE SLIME ESCAPE HAS BEEN GOOD FOR EVERYONE.

EVERYONE EXCEPT MR. SNAG!

Their laughter echoed down the hall, all the way to the school's front door.

"Did you hear that?" Tank hissed. "Rizzo's dad is selling tons of vacuum cleaners because of that stupid anti-slime law. He's happy the slimes caused so much damage."

"Maybe he's behind their escape," I said.

The walls shook as another tremor ran through the school. I grabbed the handrail. As quickly as it came, the shaking stopped.

"Did you notice that?" Tank asked.

"Kind of hard to miss," I said.

"Not the shaking, dragonbait," she said. "The noise."

"What noise? There wasn't any noise."

"Exactly! There was no boom or crash. It was like magic."

"The purple dust!" I said.

"Someone is using the purple dust to make silent explosions."

"That's why the school is shaking so much!"

We hurried down the stairs. The basement was cold and silent. We saw no sign of Mr. Zallin. That wasn't a surprise. The caretaker was always busy at lunchtime, mopping up spills and sweeping up dropped sandwiches.

The basement shook with another tremor. Rock dust drifted down from cracks in the ceiling. The shaking was getting worse. Still there was not a sound.

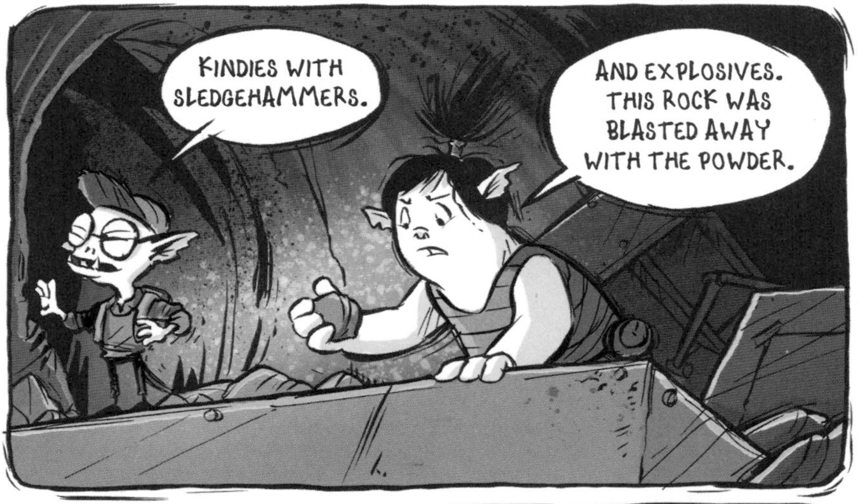
KINDIES WITH SLEDGEHAMMERS.
AND EXPLOSIVES. THIS ROCK WAS BLASTED AWAY WITH THE POWDER.

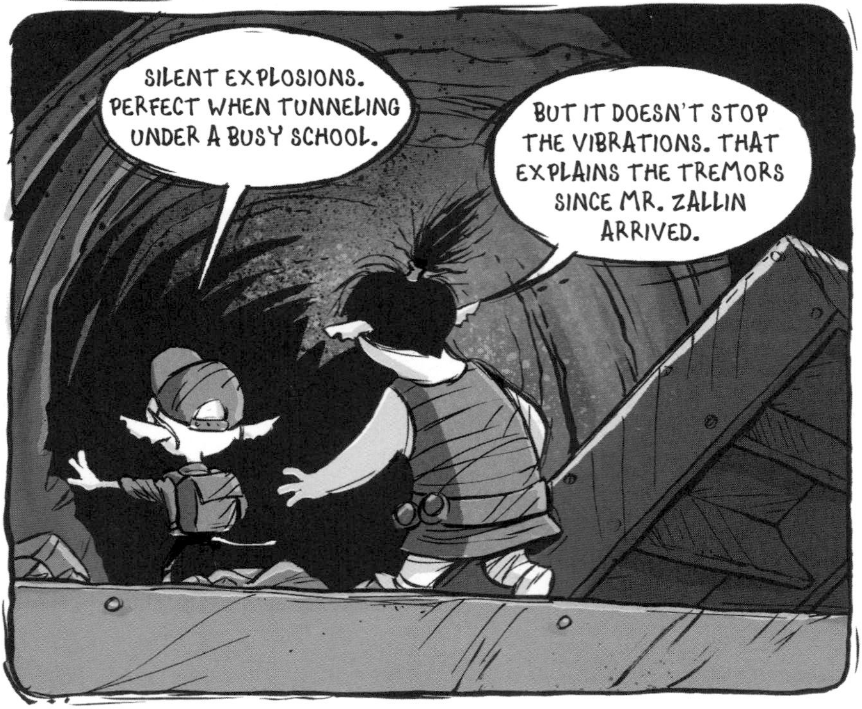
SILENT EXPLOSIONS. PERFECT WHEN TUNNELING UNDER A BUSY SCHOOL.
BUT IT DOESN'T STOP THE VIBRATIONS. THAT EXPLAINS THE TREMORS SINCE MR. ZALLIN ARRIVED.

We had only just stepped into the tunnel when the walls began to shake. Another tremor rocked through the school. Behind me, in Zallin's office, tools rattled along his desk. Something heavy fell to the floor, landing with a loud crash. The shaking was much worse down here, but still there was no boom or loud noise.

"That's the third tremor today," Tank said. "That's the most we've had in a day."

The tunnel was longer than I had first thought. We trudged through the darkness without speaking.

I pulled the jar of slime out of my pack.

"Little Scrapper isn't glowing," I said. "I don't think our slime radar is working."

"Stop!" Tank grabbed my shoulder. "Did you hear that?"

Something heavy scraped along the tunnel behind us. We froze.

There it was again. Footsteps on stone.

Getting closer.

"Someone's coming," Tank whispered.

CHAPTER SIXTEEN
Cloak and Swagger

The footsteps got louder. And closer. Whatever was coming was moving fast.

I spied a small crevice in the wall. It was barely big enough for a goblin. I jumped in anyway. Tank pushed in behind me. She didn't get far.

"I don't fit!" she hissed, stumbling back into the tunnel. "Hold on. Let me get something."

She rummaged through the pockets on her tool belt.

PLEASE, NOT THE TICKLEBOT.

GET IN HERE OR GET OUT.

MAKE SOME SPACE SHORTY!

?

We waited until the sound of its voice had faded before tumbling out of our hiding spot.

"That was close," I gasped.

"Too close." Tank hastily folded the piece of fabric.

"What is that thing? A new invention? Some kind of mechanical camouflage barrier?"

Tank shook her head. "My raincoat. Mom always makes me pack one."

"Your raincoat! You planned to save us with your raincoat?"

"You're the one who pulled me into that bug hole!" Tank stared at something over my shoulder. "Your backpack is glowing." A soft green light showed through the material of my bag.

"Little Scrapper!" I opened my backpack. Safe inside its little container, the slime glowed a calm green. Hutch was right. This thing could sense Snag's slimes. "We're getting close."

A newfound sense of confidence washed over me. I held Little Scrapper's container close to my chest. Ahead, the tunnel opened to a wide cavern. We crept to the entrance and peered inside.

Little Scrapper lit the cavern wall with a soft glow. The rocks were jagged and sharp, like they'd been hacked out by a blind ogre with a pickax. Bits of pulverized rock lay everywhere. A haze of purple dust floated in the air.

In the middle of the cavern, a blue creature smaller than me skipped around the room, singing.

"Boom, boom! We make room! Boom, boom! Treasure be ours soon!"

It was the monster that had skipped past us. It had large fat ears and a tail that ended in a sharp spike. I'd seen a lot of different monsters in Slick City, but I'd never seen one of these creatures.

On second thought, maybe I had.

"Gremlins," I said. Icy claws ran down my spine, gripping me all the way to my tail.

"We've found the Gremlin Gang," Tank said in a whisper almost too quiet to hear.

The Gremlin Gang had arrived in Slick City. Mom had said they were on their way here.

It didn't make sense. Slick City had banks with stacks of money and galleries with priceless works of art. And yet, here was the Gremlin Gang, right under my school.

The gremlin stopped singing and charged to a dark corner of the cavern. He returned with a heavy-looking bucket. He zipped to the middle of the cave and climbed a ladder standing beneath a shallow hole in the ceiling. The ladder looked familiar. On its side were the words *Property of Gravelmuck Elementary*.

"That ladder is from the school!" I said.

"They're a gang of antique thieves," Tank whispered. "Stealing a battered old school ladder is not going to bother them."

The gremlin teetered at the top of the ladder. One hand carried the bucket. The other held a large paintbrush. He dipped the brush in the can. It came out covered in purple paint. Purple, sparkling paint.

"The purple dust!" Tank said. "It's in the paint."

The gremlin spread the paint on the ceiling of the cavern. He hopped off the ladder and dragged it to the far corner. He turned to face the hole in the ceiling and got that look of concentration I'd only ever seen on Aleetha. The gremlin said the same magic words Aleetha had used at the harbor.

The dust on the ceiling bubbled. It shook.

I grabbed the wall. I knew what was coming.

The patch of purple paint exploded. Rocks flew from the ceiling. The entire tunnel shook. It all happened without making a sound.

"That proves the purple dust is the source of the tremors," I said when my brain had stopped shaking.

"The Gremlin Gang is using the dust to make a tunnel in the rock silently. No one at the school can hear it. But they can't hide the shaking."

It made sense. But something else tugged at the back of my brain.

"Why is Principal Weaver telling everyone it's the heaters shaking the school?"

"Because I told her to."

We spun around to see the owner of the voice behind us.

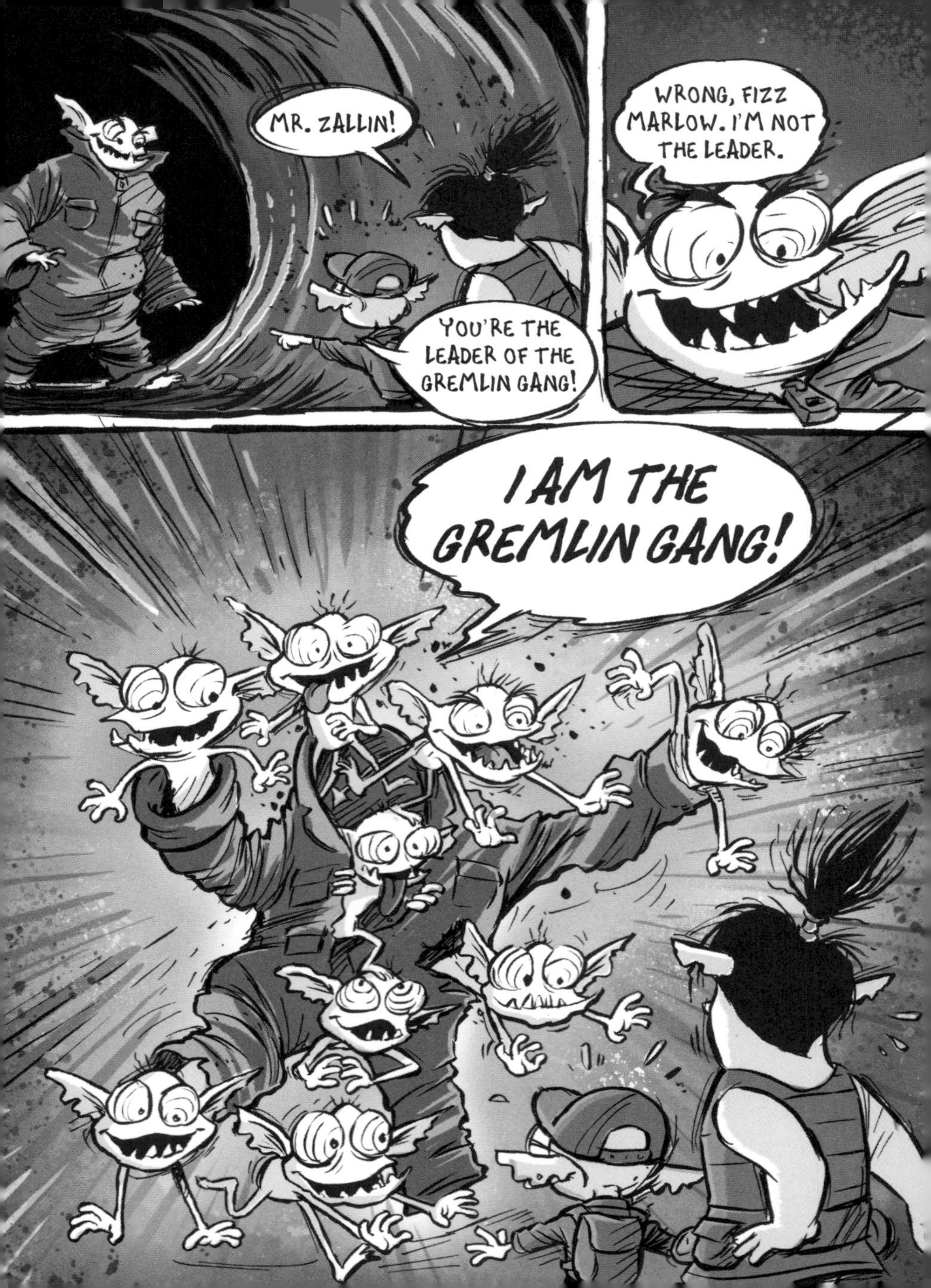
MR. ZALLIN!
YOU'RE THE LEADER OF THE GREMLIN GANG!
WRONG, FIZZ MARLOW. I'M NOT THE LEADER.
I AM THE GREMLIN GANG!

Gremlins swarmed over us. Crawling, clawing and screeching little blue creatures were everywhere. Mr. Zallin wasn't a mega-gremlin—he was *made* of gremlins. They pulled my tail and yanked Tank's hair. Blue gremlins were all I could see. Then everything went dark.

CHAPTER SEVENTEEN
Hoarding the Hoard

My hands were tied tighter than a choke-viper on a sleeping mudrat. Tank was squished beside me. Her legs and arms were tied up too. Her tool belt and my backpack lay on the ground not far from our feet.

"I knew coming down here was a mistake," she grumbled.

"Really?" I said. "You couldn't have shared that with me earlier?"

She didn't respond.

I yanked on my ropes, but that only made them tighter.

Cold rock pressed against my back. We were still in the large cavern. My head felt like it'd been dunked in a barrel of gooey slick.

Blue shapes danced in front of me. About a dozen of them. The Gremlin Gang. Here, in our school.

Our new caretaker, Mr. Zallin, had really been the entire Gremlin Gang in disguise. That's why he always walked like he was falling apart. Under those coveralls, a bunch of gremlins squished together, moving like a single monster. And it worked. They had everyone fooled, including Principal Weaver.

Now, with their disguise gone, the gremlins giggled and skipped around the cavern. The largest gremlin stood on a rock and barked orders at the rest of the gang. He had Mr. Zallin's fierce red eyes and large ears. He had been Mr. Zallin's head, sitting on the shoulders of the other gremlins. With his magical ogre disguise gone, I knew I'd seen his real face before.

Tank gave her ropes another good yank. They were tied up tight.

"It's no use," she said, slumping against the rock. "We can't do anything stuck here."

The gremlins had stopped the cart where a patch of rock had just been blasted away. All that remained of the cave ceiling were slabs of flat black rock.

"I don't get it," Tank said. "Why would a criminal gang try to rob a boring old elementary school?"

"They're not robbing the school," I said. While Tank had been pulling on her ropes, my brain had been tugging at another problem. I'd seen those slabs of black rock somewhere before. "They're robbing Mr. Trellik."

"The old troll who hates kids?" Tank said.

I nodded. "We're underground, so that ceiling is somebody's floor. Those black stones are obsidian. And there's only one place nearby that has obsidian floors."

"Trellik's Treasures antique shop!" Tank said. A little too loudly, because all the gremlins turned to look at us.

"The big goblin has figured it out. Finally." Snatch cackled.

"Who you calling a goblin?" Tank snapped. "No offense, Fizz."

The gremlins positioned the slimes beneath the obsidian. As soon as the beasts noticed the dark stone, they stretched their gooey bodies up and out of the container.

"They can sense the obsidian!" I said. "Slimes can't resist that stuff."

Snag's slimes wobbled as they stretched up toward the obsidian. Their tips touched the stone and attached. With amazing strength, the slimes pulled the rest of their goopy bodies up to the obsidian. In seconds, they were munching away on the rock. They began to dissolve it with their powerful acids.

The gremlins cackled and danced in circles, chanting.

"Eat the stone! Eat the stone! Soon the treasure will be ours alone!"

"They're after Firebane's Hoard," Tank said. "The slimes are eating their way into Mr. Trellik's antique shop."

"All those valuable treasures would be irresistible to a bunch of thieving gremlins."

"And we're stuck here!" Tank growled. She kicked my backpack in frustration.

The front pocket of the pack fell open. A bright green glow pulsed out from inside the bag.

My heart beat faster. A chance for escape.

I kicked my legs at the bag. A small clear container tumbled out.

"Little Scrapper!" Tank whispered.

The little slime glowed bright green. It pushed against the lid of its box.

"It senses the other slimes," Tank said. "It wants to be free."

"Maybe it can help us get free too."

I twisted my body so that I could grab the box with my hands still tied behind my back.

Snatch and the rest of the Gremlin Gang were busy watching the slimes devour the obsidian. They had forgotten all about us. For now.

My fingers ran along the edges of the cube, searching for a way to open it. Hutch had made it look so easy. But his hands weren't tied behind his back.

"Find the hidden switch and push it," Tank said.

"I know what I have to do!" I growled under my breath. "It's actually doing it that's the hard part."

My fingers felt like sausages trying to untangle a spider web. I couldn't find the hidden switch anywhere on the box.

Panic rolled up from my belly. Snag's slimes had nearly eaten through the obsidian. We didn't have much time.

"You can do it, Fizz," Tank said, her voice soft and even. "Just breathe and let your fingers relax."

I took a deep breath and pushed the panic back down into my stomach. My fingers ran along the box. The surface was smooth. The edges were tightly bound. Except for one spot, right near the middle. I pressed the spot.

The box clicked. The lid popped open. Hutch's slime oozed out.

"You did it!" Tank whisper-cheered.

Relief rushed through me. It was cut short by the feeling of something cold and slimy on my skin.

"Don't move," Tank said.

Hutch's slime oozed down my arm. It stopped on the ropes around my wrist.

"It's not burning my skin!" I said. "Hutch was right. Slimes aren't mindless savages. They only like eating garbage and rocks."

"And ropes, thankfully," Tank said.

The little slime's acids quickly burned through the ropes around my wrist. My hands were free. I picked up a chunk of rope the slime was resting on and put it on top of Tank's ropes. Immediately, it set about dissolving her ropes.

Seconds later, Tank and I were both free.

But it was too late.

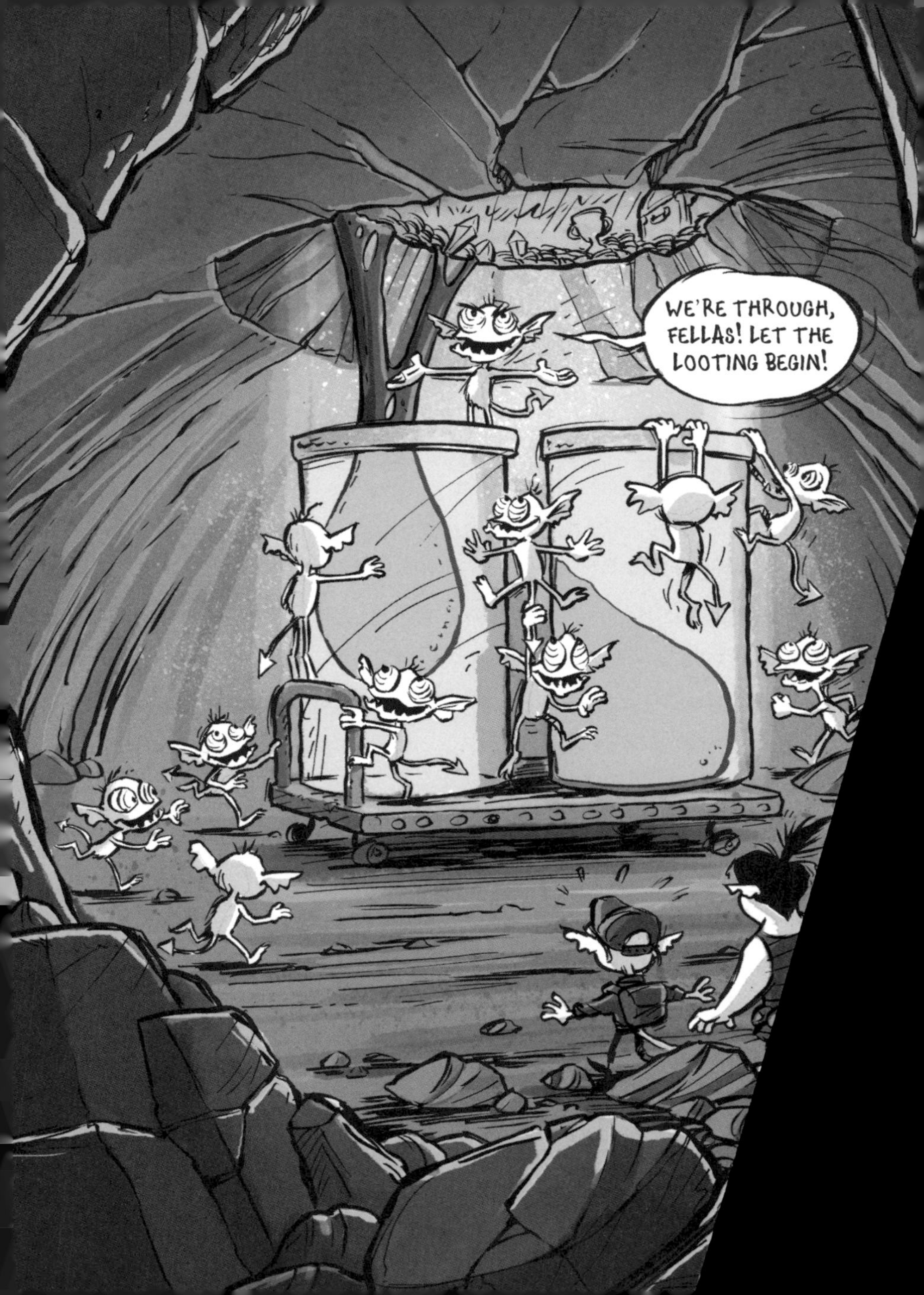
WE'RE THROUGH, FELLAS! LET THE LOOTING BEGIN!

CHAPTER EIGHTEEN
Gremlin Tea Party

Mr. Trellik's bushy head appeared over the edge of the hole.

"What is the meaning of this?" he snapped. Gremlins pushed past him and stampeded into his shop. "You can't come in here! Use the front door!" the troll ~~co~~mmanded. His teacup rattled in his hands. The grem-~~lins~~ ignored old Trellik. They bounced into the antique ~~shop,~~ knocked over display cases and stuffed anything ~~in~~to their large sacks.

~~"We're~~ too late," Tank said. "The Gremlin Gang ~~is here.~~"

~~"Say th~~at to Little Scrapper," I said.

~~I point~~ed toward the container where Snag's ~~pet dissol~~ved the chunks of obsidian inside it.

~~"Going~~ for one last snack," Tank said, ~~shrugging.~~ "I don't blame it."

"Maybe not." I scooped up Little Scrapper and dropped it onto Mr. Snag's slimes. "Hutch said Little Scrapper would send a message when we found Mr. Snag's slimes."

The slimes pulsed a rich green and melded together. They became one slime. Nothing else happened.

"Or maybe he just wants to hang out with his slime buddies," Tank said.

"I guess you're right," I said. "I was stupid to expect anything more from a mindless slime."

Glass shattered in the shop above us. Gremlins cackled at their destruction.

"That sounded expensive," Tank said.

Trellik's Treasures was a swirling mass of gremlins. They bounced off the walls. They smashed the counters. They scooped up trinkets, jewels and treasures. Their sacks bulged. They had taken nearly all of Firebane's Hoard. I looked around the tiny shop, hoping to find a treasure overlooked by the jewel-hungry gremlins. I found it against the back wall. A collection of teacups, a ceramic pot with a dragon sipping tea painted on the side and a jug of water. Tank climbed up through the hole and crouched beside me.

"Follow me," I said and raced to the back of the shop.

I figured the gremlins would be too busy filling their sacks to notice us hurrying past them.

I was wrong. A runt-faced gremlin dropped from the ceiling just as we got to the back counter.

"Where you going, goblins?" it snarled.

"I am *not* a goblin!" Tank stood up straight and growled at the runt-faced gremlin.

It stumbled back at the sight of Tank at her full height. That was all the chance I needed.

I grabbed Mr. Trellik's teapot, took off the lid and splashed hot tea into the gremlin's face. Instantly, its wet skin began to sizzle and pop. The gremlin screeched. Then its skin started turning to stone. The stone spread down the gremlin's neck and across its body. In seconds, the screeching, jumping gremlin had transformed into a statue.

"That's a neat trick," Tank said.

"Water and gremlins. A bad mix," I said.

"For the gremlins, that is." Tank grabbed the jug of water beside the cups. "Let's finish this."

We jumped over the counter and started splashing. The place was so packed with flying gremlins, we didn't have any trouble hitting them with our splashes. One by one, as their skin sizzled and popped, the gremlins turned into stone. By the time our teapot and jug were empty, all the gremlins stood frozen, turned into statues with looks of surprise on their faces.

Every gremlin, that is, except one.

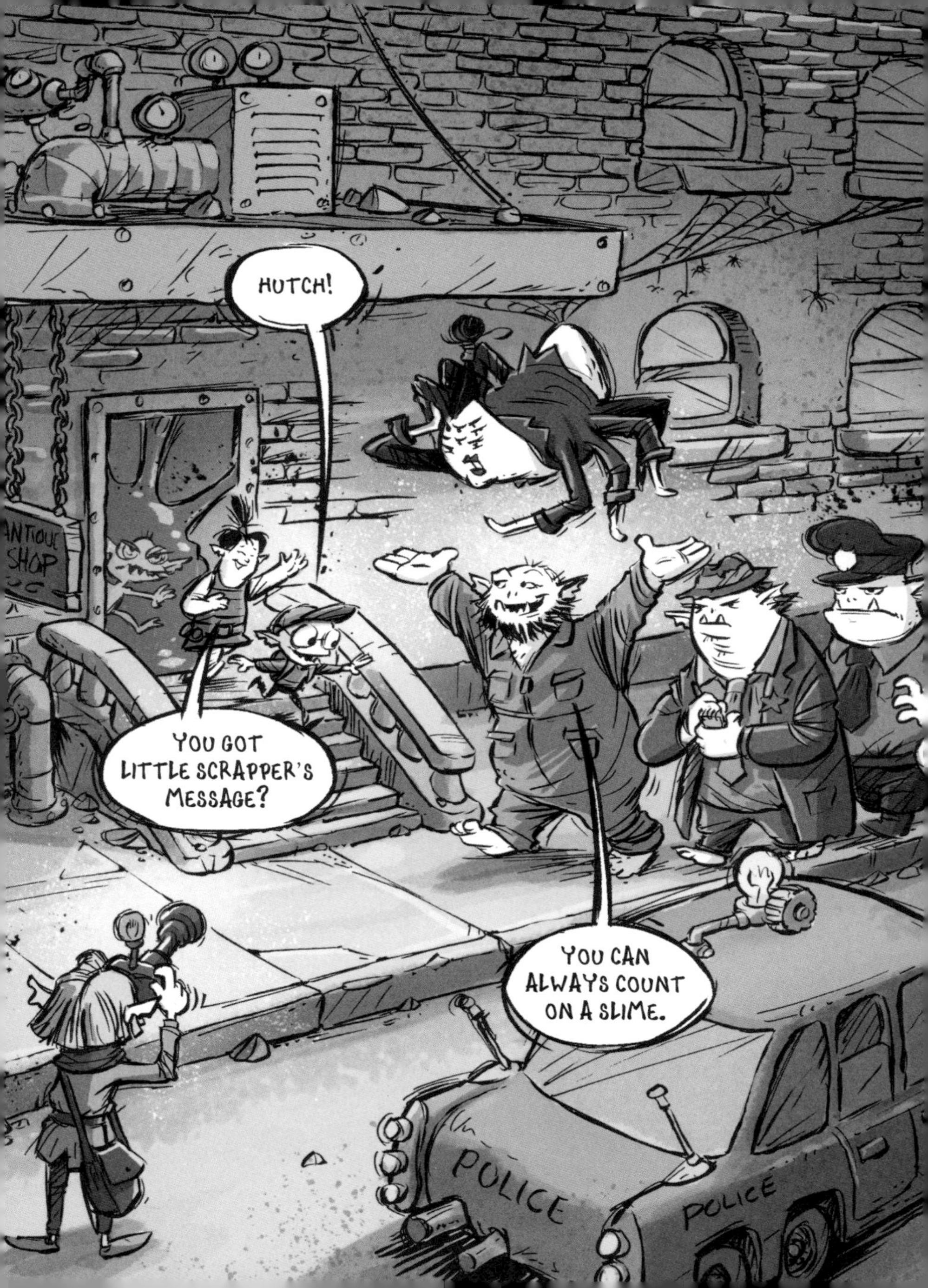
HUTCH!
ANTIQUE SHOP
YOU GOT LITTLE SCRAPPER'S MESSAGE?
YOU CAN ALWAYS COUNT ON A SLIME.
POLICE
POLICE

CHAPTER NINETEEN
Return of the Slime

The school had never looked cleaner. And Mr. Snag had never looked happier.

"There's nothing like a hallway cleaned by a slime!" The old ogre's face beamed with pride. The slimes slurped down the hallway of Gravelmuck Elementary outside Principal Weaver's office. The floor sparkled. The windows gleamed. Every part of Gravelmuck Elementary was spotless. Everything felt right.

It had been two days since Snatch and the Gremlin Gang got slimed. School had ended an hour ago and everyone had gone home. Well, almost everyone. Tank and I had stayed behind to help Mr. Snag on his first day back on the job.

Principal Weaver scuttled out of her office to inspect the slimes' handiwork. The webs in the ceiling quivered.

A few of Weaver's babies skittered out to snoop on the ogre's cleaning and our conversation.

"Very impressive, Mr. Snag," Weaver said. She did not sound impressed. In fact, she had been working hard all day to sound even a little bit happy about the old caretaker's return. She wasn't doing a very good job.

"My slimes take their job very seriously," Mr. Snag said. "And so do I."

Weaver slinked back into her office without another word. Her spider babies buried themselves into their webs, disappearing from view. That didn't mean they were not still listening to us. Weaver's spies were always listening.

"She should be happy we saved her school," Tank whispered. "Instead, she blames us for making her look silly."

"It's not our fault she was tricked by Snatch and his gremlins," I said.

After the police had pulled Snatch out of the slime, the Gremlin Gang leader had started talking. He confessed to leading his gang into Gravelmuck Elementary late one night to release the slimes. They used their magical powers to unlock the front door and let the slimes loose. Their goal was to get Mr. Snag fired so they could tunnel under the school to Mr. Trellik's shop and steal Firebane's Hoard.

Principal Weaver had known nothing about who Snatch really was or what he was doing. She was just so eager to save money, she believed everything he said about vacuum cleaners and heaters that caused the whole school to shake.

When the police had heard Snatch's confession, they'd released Mr. Snag immediately, and he'd got his job back.

"Thanks again for your help, kids," Mr. Snag said. "Without you two snooping around and not listening to your teachers, I'd still be stuck in that jail."

"Not listening is what they do best!" said a voice at the front door.

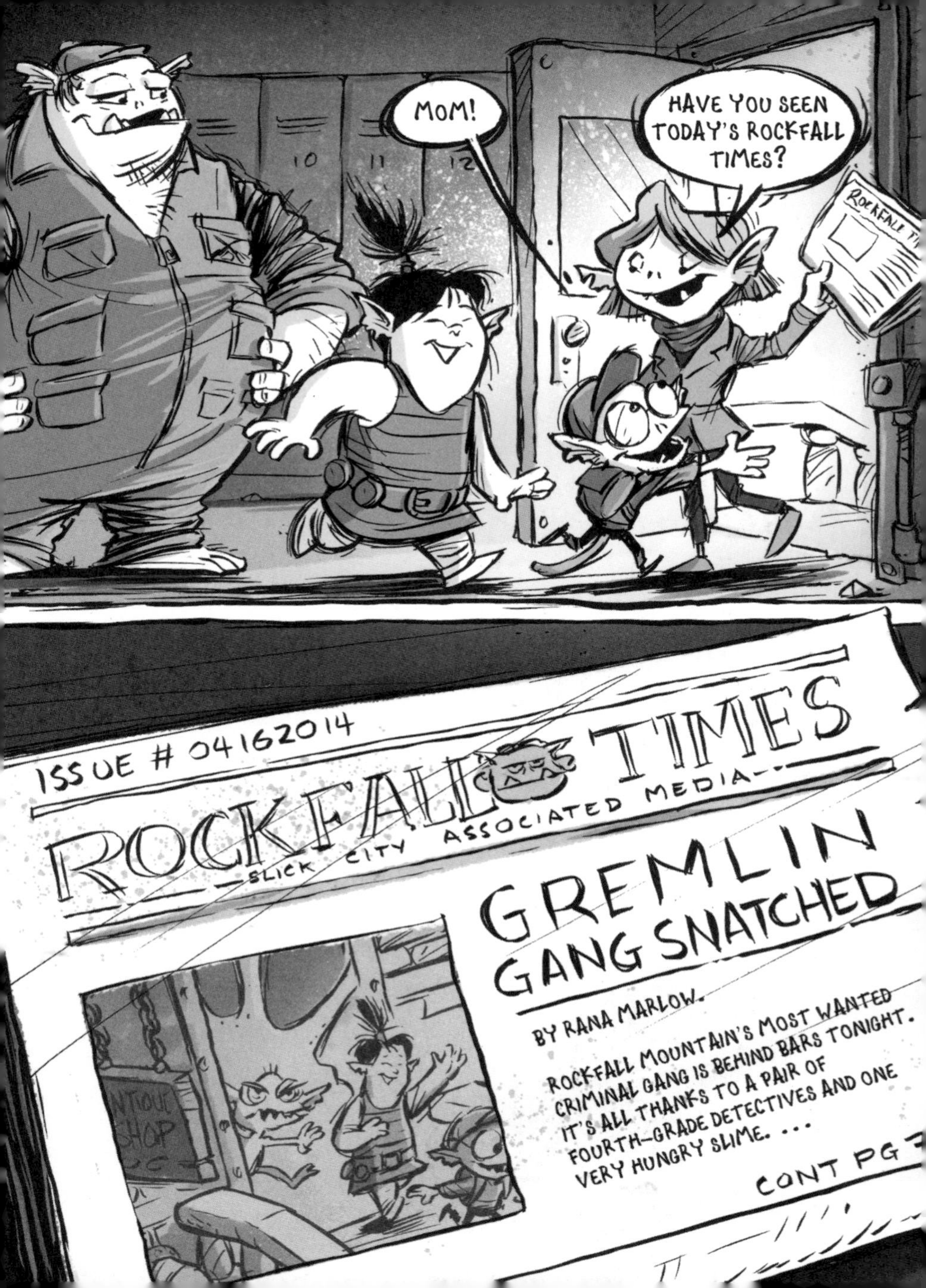

MOM!
HAVE YOU SEEN TODAY'S ROCKFALL TIMES?
ISSUE # 04162014
ROCKFALL TIMES
SLICK CITY ASSOCIATED MEDIA
GREMLIN GANG SNATCHED
BY RANA MARLOW.
ROCKFALL MOUNTAIN'S MOST WANTED CRIMINAL GANG IS BEHIND BARS TONIGHT. IT'S ALL THANKS TO A PAIR OF FOURTH-GRADE DETECTIVES AND ONE VERY HUNGRY SLIME. ...
CONT PG

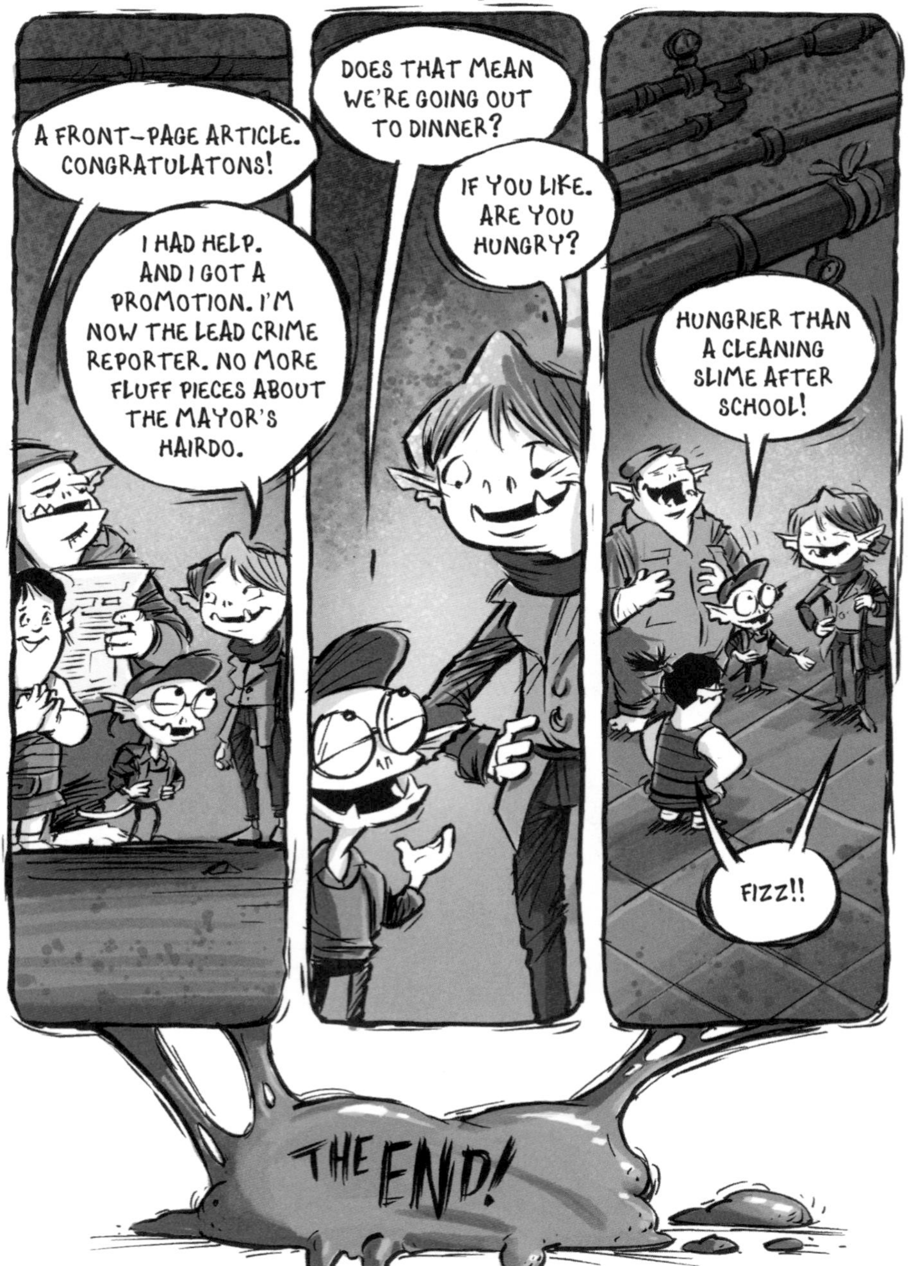
A FRONT-PAGE ARTICLE. CONGRATULATONS!
I HAD HELP. AND I GOT A PROMOTION. I'M NOW THE LEAD CRIME REPORTER. NO MORE FLUFF PIECES ABOUT THE MAYOR'S HAIRDO.
DOES THAT MEAN WE'RE GOING OUT TO DINNER?
IF YOU LIKE. ARE YOU HUNGRY?
HUNGRIER THAN A CLEANING SLIME AFTER SCHOOL!
FIZZ!!
THE END!

LIAM O'DONNELL is an award-winning children's author and educator. He's created over thirty books for young readers, including the *Max Finder Mystery* and *Graphic Guide Adventure* series of graphic novels. Liam lives in Toronto, Ontario, where he divides his time between the computer and the coffeemaker. Visit him anytime at www.liamodonnell.com or follow him on Twitter @liamodonnell.

MIKE DEAS is an author/illustrator of graphic novels, including *Dalen and Gole* and the *Graphic Guide Adventure* series. While he grew up with a love of illustrative storytelling, Capilano College's Commercial Animation program helped Mike fine-tune his drawing skills and imagination. Mike and his wife, Nancy, currently live on Saltspring Island, British Columbia. For more information, visit www.deasillustration.com or follow him on Twitter @DeasIllos.

MORE GRAPHIC NOVELS

FROM LIAM O'DONNELL AND MIKE DEAS

978155143880I • $9.95 PB

JUNIOR LIBRARY GUILD SELECTION

978155143756? • $9.95 PB

"Deas' illustrations are full of life."
—*Quill & Quire*